A TOOT HANSELL CHRISTMAS CRACKER

A BEAUFORT SCALES COLLECTION

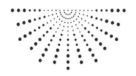

KIM M. WATT

For further information contact: www.kmwatt.com

Cover design: Monika McFarland, www.ampersandbookcovers.com

Editor: Lynda Dietz, www.easyreaderediting.com

Logo design by www.imaginarybeast.com

ISBN: 978-1-8383265-3-1

First Edition: December 2020

10 9 8 7 6 5 4 3 2 1

To you, lovely reader.
You made it through 2020.
*That sort of courage deserves **all***
the dragons and baked goods.

Keep going, lovely people.
You got this.

A BEAUFORT SCALES MYSTERY

CRACKER (NOUN):

Pronunciation /ˈkrakə/

1. A decorated paper cylinder which, when pulled apart, makes a sharp noise and releases a small toy or other novelty.
'A Christmas cracker'

2. *British informal* A fine example of something.
'A cracking meal.'

- from the Oxford English Dictionary (online)

There are other definitions, of course, but the ones which apply to hacking code or dealing with hydrogen bonds are of rather less relevance here. Although the one involving savoury biscuits for eating with cheese would fit fairly well too ...

2020 has been *a year.* It's hit all of us in different ways, to a greater or lesser extent, and I don't think anyone has been unaffected by it.

I also don't think any of us would describe it as a cracker. Other than it bearing a certain similarity to that moment when you're waiting for the Christmas cracker to *crack*. For ten months or so.

But it hasn't been all bad. We've seen communities pull together, neighbours looking out for each other, and key workers from shop staff to frontline medical teams go to astonishing lengths to get us through this. There have been breakthroughs in medical research and huge changes how we work and live – some for the better. We've embraced sourdough, and whipped coffee, and Zoom dates, and dressing up to put the bins out, and discovered that pyjamas really are a legitimate style choice.

And however we've got through it – whether we taught ourselves guitar or mastered headstands or just built a blanket fort and have yet to emerge – we've made it.

And that, lovely people, is astounding. I'm in awe of you all. And this particular Christmas cracker is for you - I hope it brings you as much escapism (and baked goods overload) in the reading as it did me in the writing.

Look after yourselves out there.

Kim x

PS: A little note on the recipes. I work in metric, and generally by weight, so although I have endeavoured to offer conversions here, I will freely admit that I became slightly bewildered by the variety of ways things *could* be converted (butter can be measured in ounces, cups, tablespoons, and *sticks*? What sticks? Are we talking broomsticks or Pooh-sticks here?).

As such, and also because my baking tends toward the cavalier, if things seem *really* out you might want to check with your friendly search engine.

But I have tried.

And if you prefer to keep your book clean, if you head to the back you'll be able to download all the recipes in a handy ebook.

Happy baking!

CONTENTS

1

A PARTRIDGE IN A PEAR TREE

R ose lifted the rum bottle to eye level and scowled at it. Despite such overt intimidation, it remained resolutely empty – or near enough so. There was a teeny bit left, the sort of reluctant splash left behind when one didn't want to be seen to actually finish the bottle. She grumbled and looked at Angelus, sprawled on the stone floor of the kitchen with his long legs going every which way.

"Who did it?" she asked him. "I bet it was bloody Campbell. Invite him over for a coffee and he stays half the weekend and drinks all my rum."

Angelus thumped his tail but offered no opinion on the matter. Which, she supposed, was only to be expected. Campbell had brought a new toy in the shape of a Christmas gnome with a squeaker that played "Jingle Bells". Angelus adored it, and so would not be betraying Campbell. Rose, however, had had to hide the thing in the log store to stop herself throwing it in the fire.

Then again, she admitted to herself as she tipped the dregs of rum into her coffee cup, there *was* the possibility, however small, that she'd finished it herself. It was the festive season, after all, and what better than a little spiced rum to warm things up?

THE FESTIVE ADDITION to her coffee was rather pleasant, but didn't solve the problem that she had at least another four batches of rum and raisin truffles to make for the winter market, and no rum to make them with. And while rumless truffles might still be *acceptable* truffles, it rather took the fun out of things. So she put Angelus on his leash, shrugged into her biggest winter coat to guard against the narrow wind scratching at the doors, and headed into town. The Toot Hansell village shop might not exactly stock premium spirits, but it was better than driving all the way to Skipton.

After a brisk jaunt around the village green (avoiding the duck pond, as the geese seemed particularly agitated at the moment, and the ducks had withdrawn to the grass to splash sulkily in puddles), Rose found herself examining two bottles which contained something that *looked* like rum. She wasn't sure how far the resemblance extended, however.

"What's 'rum-inspired' meant to mean, then?" she asked the shopkeeper, who shrugged. He was wearing a green jumper with red baubles knitted into it that had seen far too many Christmases.

"I suppose it means that they've taken inspiration from rums around the world in order to create an ultimate rum blend," he said.

"I don't want an ultimate rum blend. I just want rum. For truffles," she clarified, in case he thought she was having a party and tried to get himself invited.

"That one's rum," he said, pointing a greasy finger at the other bottle. Rose could still smell the bacon butty he must've had for breakfast. She examined the second bottle more closely.

"It's rom," she said. "With an O."

They looked at each other for a moment, then the shopkeeper shrugged again and said, "You could always go to Skipton."

"Ugh." Rose examined the bottles and sighed. "No, these will just have to do. I'll take them both."

"Really?" he asked, then corrected himself. "I mean, of course. That'll be fifty quid."

Rose just looked at him.

"Forty," he offered.

She tapped her gloved fingers on the counter, and he groaned.

"Thirty-five," he said. "And only because you're taking both."

"Daylight robbery," she announced. "I bet you paid about two quid a bottle for them." But she bought them anyway. She couldn't make truffles without rum. And one of them would have to be palatable. She hoped.

THE MYSTERIOUS RUM-INSPIRED blend made her eyes twitch, and the rom made them water, but having sampled both of them Rose concluded that no one was really that likely to complain about it. Not once the alcohol was soaked into dried fruit and balanced with dark chocolate and coconut and biscuit. And with a couple of weeks still to go before the market, it gave the flavours plenty of time to mellow. So she stirred a little of each rum into a new batch of chopped raisins, then went back to the mix she'd made earlier and left to rest in the fridge, forming spoonfuls into neat, tight balls before rolling them in more coconut and placing them in haphazard ranks on trays to firm up properly. Her fridge was too full to keep them in there, but the old porch with its leaking window frames was more than cold enough to do the trick. She'd pop them in jars tomorrow, and replace them with the next batch.

She bounced happily to the radio as she worked, a small

woman with white hair and skinny, slightly knobbly wrists, and Angelus snored by the rickety cooker, and outside the wind blew but inside all was warm and filled with scent.

Rose hadn't intended to fall asleep on the sofa, but it appeared the rum-inspired-rom mix was rather stronger than she'd antici-pated. That, and the rather inexplicable urge to nap that had started to overcome her sometime around her eightieth birthday. It was ridiculous. All she'd been doing was *cooking*, for heaven's sake. She sat up, yawning, pottered through to the kitchen with Angelus trailing her faithfully, and peered into the garden. The early winter dusk had already settled, rendering the bushes dull and the trees skeletal, and everything was painted in shades of cold grey.

She needed logs for the fire, so she pulled her jacket on, still half-asleep, and wandered through the porch to grab the wheel-barrow resting against the wall outside and head down the garden to the log store. A sharp, stinging drizzle had started, and it peppered her cheeks, making her blink and gasp, shaking off the last of the sleepiness. Angelus tore off around the garden as if he'd never seen it before, and she stopped to watch him, smiling as he took a rose bush for a mortal enemy and barked at it hysterically. Then he spotted something else and went to roll in it, and she had to abandon the wheelbarrow, running down the garden and shouting at him to stop. That was the last thing she needed – having to wash fox poo off a Great Dane just before dinner. Angelus saw her coming, yelped, and took off again, his legs flailing as he slipped on the wet ground, and she stopped, shaking a finger at him.

"No rolling! *No rolling*, Angelus!"

A *whuff* answered her from somewhere in the veggie garden, and she gave up, returning to the wheelbarrow and carrying on to the log store. She half-filled the barrow, careful not to dislodge the hidden chew toy and set off a squawky chorus of "Jingle Bells", then carted the logs back to the house, shouting for Angelus as she went.

She was carrying the first load of logs into the house when she stopped in the porch, staring at the trays of truffles. She hadn't exactly had them in military rows, but now there seemed to be *gaps,* as if someone had grabbed them up in great handfuls. She dumped the logs, shaking the trays to spread out the truffles and counting rapidly, trying to remember how many she usually got out of each batch. More than this. *Definitely* more than this.

"Angelus!" she shouted, the word catching in her throat. "Angelus, come here!" But he'd been inside. The door had been shut when she woke up. He *couldn't* have— *"Angelus!"* She almost screamed his name, and then he was there, beaded with rain, tail wagging gently as he stared at her.

"Did you?" she demanded, pointing at the trays. "Did you eat them?"

He cocked his head at her, and she grabbed his collar, dragging him into the house and away from the truffles, searching for her phone. Her heart was going far too fast for comfort.

THE VET WAS STILL OPEN, and Rose made the twenty-minute drive in under fifteen. She piled into the reception area dragging a reluctant, whining Angelus behind her, and was halfway to the desk before he decided he wasn't having any of it. He braced his feet on the doormat, trying to pull away, and Rose's boots slipped on the slick flooring. She yelped, and a man sitting in the plastic reception chairs leaped up to help her pull the Great Dane in. The cat hunched in the carrier next to his seat spat at all of them, then yawned.

"He's eaten chocolate," Rose told the veterinary nurse at the counter. "Or I think he has. Also rum. And raisins."

"Jesus," the man said, and the cat made a sound that was oddly like a snicker.

Rose gave them both a cold look. "Rum and raisin truffles. They were outside, but some are missing."

"Was he outside?" the veterinary nurse asked.

"No," Rose admitted. "But I don't think anything else could've taken them."

"Alright," he said. "Let's get you checked out."

For a moment Rose thought the nurse was talking to her rather than Angelus, and was about to say she hoped he wasn't referring to her age, then he came out from behind the counter and led her into the treatment rooms.

Rose was almost certain she heard the cat say, "Jumping the damn queue. Typical bloody dogs."

IT WAS ALMOST dinnertime when they got home, a rather subdued Angelus following Rose into the house. After weighing the Great Dane, and with some guesswork on Rose's part regarding how many truffles were missing, the vet had decided it was unlikely, even if he had eaten any, that it was enough to do serious harm. But, just to be on the safe side, they'd sat there in the reception area until the vet went home, waiting to see if Angelus took a turn for the worse. He didn't, though. He just split his time between trying to sneak the jar of dog treats off the counter and stealing toys off the display.

Now she emptied a tin of food into his bowl and frowned at

him while he wolfed it. "You certainly don't seem poorly," she said. He ignored her, except for wagging his tail a little harder, and she sighed. Maybe she'd overreacted. Maybe he hadn't eaten *any* of the truffles, and she'd just thought he had. Maybe she hadn't actually made as many as she'd thought, or she'd dropped some, or even eaten them herself.

She rubbed her forehead, and took her glasses off to polish them. She'd lost her keys for three days last week, and Miriam had eventually found them in a jar of chutney. And she'd found a gardening glove in a loaf of bread she'd baked the week before that, which she was still mystified by. She wasn't sure how worried she should be. A *little* dottiness was to be expected, but was this too much? Was there some sort of official scale for these things, from harmless eccentricity to "call the care home"? Did she even want to know if there was?

She put her glasses back on and went to bring the truffles in. She may as well put them away before she scared herself again. And got another hefty vet's bill.

The light from the kitchen door washed through the porch, catching the spiderwebs in the corners and her muddy boots huddled under the bench. The wheelbarrow still sat outside, and logs were spilled over the floor where she'd dropped them. She'd have to get those in, too. But truffles first. She blinked, and stepped into the porch, staring down at the trays, then went back to look in the kitchen. Angelus was chasing his bowl across the floor, apparently convinced that if he licked it enough, more food would materialise. Rose turned back to the trays. They were empty but for a light coating of abandoned coconut.

"Oh," she said, and started picking the wood up instead. They had been nearly full when she went to the vet. They *had*. She was sure of it.

Almost.

ROSE LAY IN THE DARK, staring up at the ceiling, ignoring Angelus' snores from the side of the bed. The trays had been full, then a few had gone, then while she was at the vet the rest had gone. She wasn't confused about it. She hadn't *forgotten*. Or she didn't think she had.

She sat up with a sigh and swung her feet off the bed, grabbing the big poncho she used as a dressing gown and padding downstairs barefoot. Angelus didn't even move. Some guard dog he was. In the kitchen, she put the kettle on and fished the tea out of the cupboard, watching her hands as she did so. The fingers were still quick, even if the joints hurt some mornings and the skin was loose and fine over the bones. There was no escaping getting older, she thought. And it was nothing to regret, really, but … she just wished she knew what had happened with the truffles.

Sighing, she set the rom-soaked raisins to drain and pulled the chocolate from the cupboard. No point crying over lost truffles.

BY THE TIME Rose sat down for breakfast she'd rolled two more trays of truffles, setting them on the high shelf that ran around the porch (after removing an astonishing amount of spiders, three empty plant pots, and a rather dashing hat she'd liberated from a half-forgotten boyfriend and then lost years ago. It still looked better on her than it had on him). She'd also made neat, handwritten labels for the jars she intended to put the truffles in, including a small but clear warning that these truffles were rather more suited to adults than children, especially if consumed in quantity. The whole kitchen smelled of spice and melted chocolate, and she hummed to herself quietly as she spread marmalade on her toast, Angelus watching her carefully. Robins were congregating on the bird feeder outside, skittish in the thin morning light. They flitted back and forth without wanting to settle, and Rose frowned at them, wondering if there was a cat in the garden, and whether cats were particularly partial to truffles.

And then there was a noise from the porch, small but most certainly not robin-like. It wasn't all that cat-like, either. In fact, it sounded very much like the creak the bench gave when she sat on it to take her boots off. Angelus looked around, his ears twitching, and Rose slipped off her chair and crept to the door. She curled her fingers around it, then jerked it open with a shout of, *"Ha!"*

Well, that was the plan, anyway, but that particular door could be sticky, and it didn't open on the first try, so she just jolted her shoulder and shouted, *"Ha!"* at the blank back.

"Dammit," she mumbled, and jiggled the handle until the door opened and she could peer into the porch. The trays of truffles were still balanced on the high shelf, but there were damp footprints on the wooden bench and the grey stone flags of the porch floor. Very distinctive footprints, too.

"Ha," she said again, with a certain amount of satisfaction (and no small measure of relief because, missing keys aside, this meant she *wasn't* dotty, or not about the truffles, anyway). She pulled her boots on, shutting Angelus in the sweet-smelling kitchen, then went to stand at the edge of the porch, the day dawning grey and dull about her as she examined the garden. Her gaze settled on the old pear tree near the veggie patch. It hadn't given her any pears for years, but it cast a nice bit of shade on the nearby bench in the summer. It seemed a shame to get rid of it just because it wasn't as productive as it once had been.

Rose put her hands in her pockets and walked down to the pear tree, stopping beneath it to look up into the bare branches.

"Morning," she said. There was no answer, and she sighed. "I had to take Angelus to the vet. I thought he'd eaten the truffles."

Heavy eyelids the colour of the scabbed grey bark opened, and milky eyes regarded her. "Is that that monstrous dog of yours? He chased me last night."

"So he should," she said. "You ate three trays of truffles. *Three!*"

The dragon sniffed and said, "I couldn't reach the others. You put them up too high."

"You weren't meant to reach them. They're not for you."

"Then why were they outside?"

"To cool off." Rose frowned at him. "Do get down, Walter. My poor old tree doesn't need a dragon sitting in it."

Walter sighed and uncoiled himself, dropping heavily to the ground. His talons tore divots in the wet earth, and he shook himself, scattering rain everywhere. His wings were a bit on the ragged side, and his scales had the patchy, ill-fitting look of a lizard that has lost its tail and grown a new one that doesn't quite match. Rose wasn't sure just how old Lord Walter was, but it seemed to her that he wasn't the sort to go in for ageing gracefully. He sat back on his haunches, scraped a raisin from between his teeth, and said, "Do you have any milk?"

"I'm sorry?"

"Milk. There's usually some to wash things down with. Or brandy. Brandy'd be better. Damn cold out here."

"There's usually milk?" Rose asked, wondering if Walter was the one going a bit dotty.

"With the cake. Sometimes biscuits. And carrots, although gods know why. I'm not a bloody rabbit."

She looked at him for a long moment, then said, "Cake and milk."

"Yes. Or brandy, as I say. Do you have some?"

"You go around stealing cake and brandy from people's doorsteps."

"Sometimes hearths," he said. "And it's not *stealing*. It's tradition."

"A *Christmas* tradition?" she asked.

"Well, it's older than the whole Christmas thing, but these days, yes." He shook his scruffy wings out and yawned. "Yours was a bit early, but no complaints here. I normally keep an eye on things from early December. Don't want anyone leaving stuff out too long and attracting pixies. Damn nuisance, they are."

"But why would people be leaving cake out for you?" Rose asked.

"I said. It's tradition. People used to leave offerings for local dragons all the time, but now they only remember around Christmas. Sometimes it's not till Christmas *Eve*. It's just laziness."

For one moment Rose considered explaining who the milk (or brandy) and mince pies were really left for. But Walter sat there on the drenched grass, scratching one ear with a back paw and dislodging old, dull scales that floated to the ground like crystallised feathers, the folds of his ancient skin hanging from his shoulders and his eyes dim but *alive*, and she didn't. Because old things are too often forgotten, too often dismissed, and she couldn't imagine what it must be to watch your entire kind fade from the world. To see them fall from being feared and respected to become nothing more than myth, relegated to stories for children.

But she did know, a little, what it is to be made small and dim by the passage of time, to fade from the notice of those who value only what's young and new. And, in her opinion, it was completely unreasonable and not to be stood for.

So she just said, "Haven't you heard of sharing? What if another dragon came along and wanted some?"

Walter snorted. "They wouldn't. I'm the only one who bothers to uphold old traditions. I even leave gifts."

Rose looked around pointedly.

"Well, I don't have any *with* me. It's only the start of December!"

Rose snorted. "Tea?" she said, turning back to the house. "I've even got some rum-inspired-rom."

"What's that when it's at home?" Walter asked, following her.

"Strong," she said.

"Well, that'll hit the spot. Good for the old joints, you know."

"I know," she said, and led the old dragon out of the dreary morning and into the warmth of the kitchen, which smelled of toast and tea and all the small special magics of the world.

ROSE'S ROM & RAISIN TRUFFLES

When I was a very small thing, my mum used to make these truffles every Christmas. Well, not these exactly, but as close as I've been able to recreate. I was never allowed more than one, as, like Rose, she firmly believed one could not make truffles without rum, and they were therefore distinctly boozy. As was my grandmother's trifle, which I was also only allowed a small serving of. I mean, officially. As a small quiet child with a very sweet tooth, I'm sure I sneakily partook of far more than my allowed portion.

Now I think about it, it's possible they both knew how to get the smaller Christmas guests to bed early ...

However, being a grown-up now (or so I'm told), I get to make my truffles exactly how I want, which in my case is non-alcoholic. And this means I can eat many of them. *Many.*

I tend to use coffee in place of rum, as the flavour really compliments the mix. But I've also used orange juice, and see no reason why chai tea or whisky or anything else that takes your fancy wouldn't work. This is actually a really flexible recipe – you could change the raisins and rum for mincemeat (there's a recipe for that later in the book), or use dried apricots and almond liqueur, or dates and coffee, or ... well, the possibilities are endless. Or at least only limited by the bounds of dried fruit. And you could swap the coconut for chopped pistachios or other nuts, too. So many options!

I have yet to perfect a decent non-alcoholic trifle, though. I'm starting to think that without the sherry, it's just a very wet, stodgy pudding. Sorry, Nana.

- 60 g / ⅓ cup raisins, roughly chopped
- 60 mL / ¼ cup rum or other liquid
- 200 g / 7 oz chocolate-coated wheaten biscuits (I use dark chocolate digestives)
- 100 g / 1 cup desiccated/shredded coconut, plus extra for rolling
- 250 g / just under 9 oz dark chocolate
- 100 g / ½ cup soft light brown sugar
- 60 mL / ¼ cup cream
- 60 mL / ¼ cup golden syrup

Marinate the raisins in the rum for about an hour.

Crush the biscuits, either in a food processor or by hand, until they're down to reasonably fine crumbs (you can fortify yourself during this strenuous activity by eating the leftover biscuits from the packet). Mix the coconut in.

Melt the chocolate, brown sugar, cream, and golden syrup in a heavy-bottomed saucepan over a low heat, stirring gently now and then. Don't overheat it, and don't worry about getting it *too* smooth – there'll be some sugar crystals remaining, but you won't notice them once everything else is in.

Add the chocolate mix and the raisin mix to the biscuits and coconut, and stir well to combine. Then refrigerate until it's still soft enough to handle, but firm enough to roll into balls (I never time this right. I usually end up hacking bits off and warming them in my hands until they're rollable).

Shape roughly tablespoon-sized scoops into balls, then roll in the extra coconut to coat. This is messy. Enjoy it.

Pop in the freezer to set and store – the flavours blend and mellow, so try and make them at least a week ahead of when you're planning to need them. They make great gifts – they don't melt, just soften a little, so you can put some in a jar and festoon with pretty ribbons, and it'll be fine to take to a friend's house. That is, if you haven't eaten them all. It's amazing how often I find myself in the freezer once I've made a batch ...

Makes ... well, 30-ish. It depends how big you roll them and how often you check the mix.

2
TWO TURTLE DOVES

Alice watched Jasmine scatter a handful of birdseed on the frosty grass, throwing it well ahead of her so that her yappy little dog Primrose didn't get too near the ducks. The ducks looked at the birdseed, then back at the two women. One gave a rather disapproving quack, and Primrose all but did backflips trying to get away from the firm grip Jasmine had on her leash.

"They're not very impressed, are they?" Alice asked.

"No," Jasmine said, spilling the packet of birdseed as she wrestled with the dog. "I think too many people still feed them bread, even though you're not meant to. Primrose, *do* stop it!"

Alice plucked the birdseed from Jasmine's hand, careful to avoid Primrose (who rolled her eyes with undeniable menace), and folded the top of the bag over. "Well, it's all you're getting," she told the ducks. They turned their backs on the women pointedly, looking at the pond where two geese were standing proudly over someone's abandoned model boat as if it were the spoils of battle. Alice supposed it was, if anyone had been silly enough to annoy the geese with it. One of the ducks gave a sound that was remarkably like a sigh, and Alice said, "Do you fancy a cup of tea at the bakery, Jasmine?"

"Ooh, yes," the younger woman said. She'd managed to disentangle Primrose from the muddle of the leash, and there were mucky paw prints all over her jeans. "Do you suppose they'll have any of those cupcakes left? The ones that look like Christmas puddings?"

"I should hope so," Alice said. "It's not even lunchtime yet." She headed across the green at a pace slow enough that Jasmine could keep up, dragging Primrose with her. The little dog was determined to escape and race back to take on the ducks, and was making it clear that she wished to remind them she was an alpha predator descended from wolves, fetching pink tartan coat notwithstanding.

Alice admired her conviction, if nothing else.

THE TOOT HANSELL village square was done up for Christmas, lights and wreaths festooning the streetlights and shopfronts, and all the shop windows glowed with cheerful displays, some of them rather more well done than others. Alice thought the hardware shop with its Nativity scene comprised entirely of power tools was a little odd, whether one believed in such things or not. Although the tiny electric drill in the manger was admittedly quite cute, somehow. Possibly due to the googly eyes on the handle.

"Look, the tree's going up," Jasmine said. "Haven't they found an enormous one this year!"

They paused to watch for a moment, Alice tucking her hands into her pockets against the chill. In addition to the huge tree (which looked as if it were going to take up half the area meant for the Christmas market by the time it was up), there was a truck with a crane on the back, and a muddy pickup truck with a closed-in tray and the council logo on the doors. Four men in hard hats and bright orange jackets milled around a big metal base, apparently arguing over how close it should be to the old well with its slate roof and bucketless winch. There was a lot of pointing and chin-scratching going on, but not a lot of anything else, and Alice didn't fancy standing around in the cold until something *did* happen. Her hip was a little achey in cold weather these days. "Shall we watch from inside?" she suggested.

"Oh, good idea," Jasmine said, and trailed after Alice into the sweet-smelling warmth of the little bakery. By the time they'd ordered at the counter, two elderly men were just leaving the table in the window, one of them tipping Alice a friendly wink as she went to claim their chairs. She considered it, then winked back and sat down. It was Christmas, after all. One could make allowances for the more harmless displays of over-familiarity.

The windowsill had been piled with a precarious display of mismatched, chipped baubles interspersed with some slightly tatty pinecones, and fairy lights hung from the frame above, reflecting a mellow glow in the glass. Jasmine sat down across from Alice, and they peered at the square through a soft haze of condensation. There was still a lot of pointing going on, but the tree was sitting firmly on the back of the truck, not moving.

"It's even bigger than last year's," Jasmine said, slipping Primrose a biscuit from her pocket. "How on earth are they going to decorate it? There can't be enough baubles!"

"Maybe they'll go for a more minimalist look," Alice said.

Jasmine wrinkled her nose. "That doesn't sound very Christmassy."

"True," Alice said. "But I hope they don't expect the Women's Institute to supply *more* decorations. We already did all the wreaths."

Jasmine made an agreeable noise and smiled at the young man carrying their cakes and tea things carefully toward them, tucking

Primrose further under the table as she did so. Wise, Alice thought. Jasmine was already banned from the tea shop after the dog had nipped the owner's ankle. Not that it was any great loss, as the tea shop always smelled inexplicably of boiled meat, and there seemed to be a faintly greasy patina to everything one touched. But Jasmine had liked it. Alice harboured suspicions it was because the tea shop owner was possibly an even worse cook than Jasmine, if there were such a thing. But still – no one deserved to be nipped by a moody Pomeranian. It wasn't civilised behaviour. She poured a little milk into her cup and checked the teapot.

"Did you see that?" Jasmine asked, leaning closer to the window and dislodging a couple of baubles. Alice grabbed them before they could set off an avalanche.

"See what?"

"There's something in the tree."

"Like a squirrel?" Alice asked, pouring the tea.

"I don't think so," Jasmine said, with the sort of concern that made Alice put the teapot down and follow her gaze. One of the orange-jacketed men seemed particularly excited, and was waving his arms about wildly. A second man was glaring at him, hands on his hips, and a third was very obviously laughing at both of them. The fourth had sat down on one of the benches and was pouring tea from a thermos flask into a plastic mug, as if he expected this to take some time to sort out. The tree, partly lifted from its cradle, leaned sadly over the square.

"There it is again," Jasmine said. "See? About halfway up."

Alice tried to follow Jasmine's pointing finger, but between the condensation on the window and the fact that the tree was far enough away that she had to admit her vision wasn't *quite* what it once was, she couldn't see much. "It's not a person, is it? It'd be just like Miriam's sister to be protesting again."

"Oh, I hope not," Jasmine said, her voice suddenly squeaky.

"She's always got that man who doesn't like wearing trousers around."

"They've left it a bit late to protest cutting the tree down, if it is them," Alice said, turning her attention back to the teapot. "I would have thought someone might have noticed people in the tree before this point, too."

"They do like wearing camouflage, though," Jasmine started, then said, *"Ooh."*

"What?" Alice looked out the window again. The shouting man was shouting so loudly now that she could faintly hear him over the murmur of the bakery customers and through the glass, and the second man was shouting back. The laughing man had sat down, and was sharing the fourth man's tea rather companionably while they waited. Alice let her gaze drift back to the tree, squinting at it.

"There," Jasmine said.

"Ah. I see," Alice said. "Oh dear. Shall we go and find out what's going on?"

"I suppose so," Jasmine said, with a longing look at her Christmas cupcake.

THEY LEFT their tea steaming gently in the cups, assuring the bakery owner they'd be back in just a moment. He looked less relieved by this than Alice felt was polite, but she didn't comment on it. She just zipped her heavy coat up again and stepped out into the chill of the day, the sky a tinny, scraped-clean blue and the shadows of the buildings deep and cold.

"I'm telling you, something *bit* me!" the first man shouted, brandishing a hairy wrist at the second man, who was holding a clipboard and wearing a battered hardhat. He stared at the first man's wrist.

"I don't see anything, Liam."

"Look! There!" Liam shoved his hand under the other's nose, making him rear back.

"Aw, it's a scratch. What, you can't handle a scratch now?" He looked at his clipboard as if he were considering making a note of it.

Liam scowled, and pulled heavy leather gloves back on. "It's a bite, Si. I know a bite when I get one. Something in that tree *bit* me."

Si shook his head, and Jasmine leaned closer to Alice, as if afraid they'd be overheard. "Do you think the man who doesn't like trousers would bite someone?"

"Barry?" Alice asked. "No. He may have philosophical objections to clothing, but I don't think he'd bite anyone."

"Unless they tried to make him get dressed, maybe," Jasmine said, and grinned.

Alice's lips twitched. "Quite. Are you certain it wasn't a squirrel, Jasmine?"

"It was too big," she said. "*Much* too big."

"How odd," Alice said, and wondered about the dragons. Not Beaufort or Mortimer, obviously, but Gilbert *had* set free an entire farm's worth of turkeys last year, among other things. He would likely be very keen on saving the trees. But he certainly wasn't the sort of dragon to bite anyone. His sister might, but she wouldn't stand for any tree-saving. Not in front of a crowd of unsuspecting humans, anyway.

Jasmine had apparently been thinking along the same lines, though, because as they watched the men put their thermos down and wander back to the truck, she said, "Could it be … you know. Something Toot Hansell-y?"

"It could be," Alice said, thinking that was a rather good way to describe the occurrences – and creatures – that had been turning up around the village ever since the Women's Institute's first encounter with dragons. As far as she knew, the ten members of the W.I. (plus two detective inspectors, due to a few criminal issues along the way) were still the only ones aware of such Toot Hansell-y aspects to the world, and the intention was to keep it that way. Some things were best to remain hidden.

"I hope it's something nice," Jasmine said. "Like, I don't know, Christmas fairies or something." She stared at the tree, her eyes bright.

"Biting ones?" Alice asked, and the younger woman's face fell.

"Oh," she said. "Oh, no – what if it's goblins again?" She pulled Primrose a little closer, and the dog huffed annoyance. "They were *awful.*"

Alice pressed a hand to her hip, the one she'd broken in her last – and, hopefully, only – encounter with goblins, and said, "I can't imagine what they'd be doing in a Christmas tree."

"True. But they definitely did bite."

The men in the truck had started the crane again, and were slowly winching the tree upright while Si waved and pointed, and Liam was stuck among the branches somewhere, apparently trying to guide it into place and cursing rather loudly. Alice was just wondering how he'd drawn the short straw when a flash of movement in the depths of the tree caught her eye.

Jasmine grabbed her arm. "There! Did you see it?"

"I think so," Alice said, shading her eyes. Whatever it had been, it was hiding again. And it had been terribly fast. Faster than a dragon. She wasn't sure how fast goblins might be. They'd seemed plenty fast enough when she met them.

"Oh, I don't like it," Jasmine said, still clinging to Alice's arm. "What if it's *worse* than a goblin? Like a … an *ogre* or something?"

"There's no point speculating," Alice said, wishing she'd brought her cane with her. Although more worrying than a pitched battle with ogres in the village square was the amount of people who were around to witness said battle. It'd be a matter of moments before it was online, and while magical Folk didn't tend to show up on camera (and, as Folk are *faint*, most people didn't even really see them, even when they were right out in the open), sometimes rumours were plenty. Enough rumours drew the wrong sort of attention, the sort that came in government vans. She looked around, wondering how on earth they were going to control the situation, and as she did there was an agonised yelp from the depths of the tree. Liam crashed out from under the branches, his hard hat askew. He was clutching his ear.

"It keeps biting me!" he yelled, and Si waved at the crane impatiently. It ground to a halt, and both the man in the cab and the one operating the crane turned to watch expectantly. Alice half-expected them to bring the tea out again.

"Calm down, lad," Si said, and Liam glared at him.

"You calm down! It's not biting *you!"* he shouted, which didn't make much sense considering Si was perfectly calm already, but Alice supposed one could be forgiven for such things when one's ear had been bitten by invisible tree monsters. She could see blood dripping onto his collar.

"Look, it's just a tree—" Si started.

"The tree isn't biting me!" Liam all but screamed. He was a rather large young man, but he reminded Alice of the children you saw when their ice cream fell off the cone. Utter betrayal of what they considered to be the natural order of things.

Si strode over to Liam and grabbed his shoulder, whether to check his ear or to shake some sense into him Alice wasn't sure, because he let go and jumped back as soon as he touched the younger man. "What the hell was *that?"*

"There it is again," Jasmine whispered. "Should we get help?"

"Who from?" Alice asked, watching the two men back away from the tree.

"The dragons?"

"It's broad daylight in the village square. I hardly think that'll help matters."

"Alright, Thompson, then."

Alice thought the world had come to a fine state when there was only a stray cat to turn to in times of crisis. "He doesn't exactly have a mobile phone, Jasmine."

She sighed. "What do we do, then?"

"We deal with it ourselves, if it comes to that." They turned their attention back to Si and Liam, who had retreated a little and were standing shoulder to shoulder, staring into the branches. Liam was still holding his ear.

"I *told* you something bit me," he said.

"It's probably a squirrel," Si said, and went to pull two shovels from the back of the pickup truck. He came back and gave one to Liam, ignoring the two men from the crane. They'd climbed onto the back for a better view and were sitting there sharing what looked like mince pies.

Si and Liam approached the tree cautiously, shovels at the ready, and Si poked the branches a few times. "Come out of there, you mangy little monster," he shouted.

"What on earth are they doing?" someone asked, and Alice looked around to see that the few people watching the tree go up had swollen to a small crowd.

"Catching a squirrel," she said, and hoped there really weren't ogres in the tree, or anything equally nasty.

Liam took a sudden swing at something. "There it is! Little sod!"

Si flailed at the branches wildly. "I got it, I got— *what the hell is that?*"

"*Get it!*" Liam shrieked, and both men attacked the tree with such enthusiasm that Alice hoped they didn't hit each other by accident. It was looking increasingly possible.

"*Oh my GOD— Hit it! Hit it, Liam!*"

Liam screeched something wordless, and they both thrashed at the branches in a blind panic, jumping as they tried to follow something unseen up the tree. Mottled browns and grey-greens moved and flowed among the shifting foliage, too fast and sleek for Alice to really make out. It was as if the tree itself were moving.

Then something burst from the shelter of the branches and hit Liam's chest with a rather determined thud. Liam yelped and dropped his shovel, staggering away from the tree and clawing at his assailant, which appeared to have attached itself firmly to his high vis jacket. Its solid, dull brown body covered most of his front, like some sort of aggressive armour plating, and he couldn't seem to shift it. He swore rather creatively as he tugged at it, setting off an *ooh* from the crowd. Si hefted his shovel like he was about to take a swipe at the thing, and Liam screamed at him not to be a pillock, which at least saved him from a shovel to the chest. Si dropped the shovel and grabbed the creature with his bare hands instead, pulling it away with the sound of tearing fabric. The creature promptly started snapping wildly at Si instead, who squawked and dropped it.

"Is that …?" Jasmine asked, barely paying attention to Primrose, who was yapping and twisting on her leash.

"I think so," Alice said. "How curious."

"Don't hurt it!" someone shouted from the crowd as Liam pulled a leg back to kick the creature, and both men hesitated, looking at each other. The creature promptly lurched forward and sank its … well, *beak*, Alice supposed, into the young man's boot. Liam kicked out like he was in a chorus line, but the creature hung on grimly, and as the young man hopped about he stepped on the shovel and sent himself crashing to the ground with a shout of fright. Si picked up his own shovel again, waving it in a vaguely threatening manner.

"Get it off!" Liam screamed, but Si didn't seem too keen on getting any closer. The two men on the truck had put down their

mince pies and climbed to the ground, hanging well back, and somewhere in the crowd someone was crying, and someone else was shouting encouragement.

"Should we do something?" Jasmine asked, and Alice nodded. Calling animal control was her first thought, but that could take rather longer than it looked like they had, considering the determination with which the creature was assaulting Liam. She started forward, wondering if turning a hose on them might be helpful, and as she did so Jasmine shouted, "Primrose, *no!*"

The little dog shot past Alice and straight into the fray, all bristling fluff and shining teeth, and Jasmine plunged after her, still shouting.

"Oh no," Alice said, and broke into a jog.

"Heel! Sit!" Jasmine yelled, sprinting over the uneven cobbles.

"Help me!" Liam shrieked at Si, and the older man took a tentative stab at the creature with his shovel. Alice very clearly heard someone in the tree say, *"Humans,"* then a second creature came hurtling out of the branches like an infuriated cannonball.

"Jasmine, watch out!" Alice shouted, and the younger woman ducked, covering her head with one arm. The creature just missed her, and Si flailed at it with his shovel, hitting it more by luck than aim. It tumbled to the cobbles, landing on its back and rocking wildly with its legs pedalling and jaws snapping before the momentum rolled it upright.

"Primrose, *come here,*" Jasmine ordered, and grabbed for the dog, but she slipped away, making little darting rushes at the second creature, which hissed warningly. Liam was untying his boot as he tried to escape the first one, and Si looked like he wanted to try hitting something with the shovel again.

Alice peered into the tree, looking for the source of the attack. For a moment there was nothing, just the deep green of the needles and the scarred grey-brown of the branches, then the whorls and knots in the wood swam slowly into focus, and two faces stared back at her. They had fissured skin and mossy hair and long, twiggy fingers, and they were both grinning broad, wooden smiles. She put her hands on her hips, glaring at them. One of them started to make a rude gesture, but the other caught their hand and nodded at the second creature on the ground as it gave Primrose a final hiss and latched onto Liam's other boot just as he slipped out of the first. They both giggled.

"*Stop this,*" Alice hissed at the tree, trying to keep her back to anyone who might see. "What on *earth* are you doing?"

"Just a little payback," one of the tree things said. Alice supposed it was a dryad, although she'd always rather assumed they were delicate, ethereal things. Then again, until recently she'd assumed they were mythical, too, so it just proved the old saying about assumptions.

"You always chop our trees down without even a thought," the dryad said. "No one even looks to see who's living in it."

Alice opened her mouth, shut it again, then said, "You're right. It's very careless. And I'm sorry. But if these people know you exist, they'll do more than kill your trees. You do realise this, don't you?"

There was silence from the tree for a moment, although Alice could hear Jasmine shouting for Primrose, and Liam shouting at Si, and the crowd still *ooh*-ing and *ahh*-ing. Then the first dryad nudged the other one and said, "Come on. Enough fun for now."

"Eh," the second one said. "That dog always wees under the willow by the river. It's doing awful things to the roots. Can't we just grab it?"

"Best not," the first said, and then they were gone, vanishing into the branches and just *gone,* leaving behind the snapping, furious creatures still assaulting Liam.

Alice turned around just in time to see Liam scrabbling back from his boots in a pair of Christmas socks while Si brandished his shovel unhelpfully and Jasmine scooped Primrose up mid-attack on the creatures. Unfortunately the dog was so excited she promptly bit Jasmine's arm, and when Jasmine dropped her she turned around and bit Liam on the leg, and the only reason she didn't bite anyone else was that she then lunged at Alice, who used her most Alice voice on her, and the dog sank to the ground and rolled over, exposing her belly to the sky.

Alice tucked silver-grey hair behind one ear and straightened her cardigan as the crowd erupted into applause.

"That was *awesome!*" someone shouted. "Are you doing it again tomorrow?" The two men still standing by the truck looked at each other, then one took off his hard hat and went to collect donations.

"YOUR DOG BIT ME," Liam said, glaring at Jasmine while one of the men from the truck bandaged his leg roughly. His ear was still bleeding.

"So did the tortoise," Jasmine said, pulling Primrose closer. "She was only trying to *help.*"

"Some help," Liam said, examining his wrist. "And they're snapping turtles, anyway, not tortoises."

Si stared at the turtles, currently roaming the bed of the pickup and snapping at each other irritably. "What were they doing in a tree? They don't climb, do they?"

"They're not even native," Liam said. "They must've been someone's pets." Everyone looked at him, and he scowled. "What? I like reptiles. I've got a chameleon and two salamanders at home."

"But in the *tree*," Si repeated. "Two turtles dove out of the *tree.*"

"Dived," Alice said. "Just because you've had a shock is no reason to get sloppy with your grammar."

Si just looked at her, then said, "In the *tree*."

"Maybe it was a tornado," Jasmine said. "You know, they got

blown up there." No one answered, and she flushed. "Well, what else could it be?"

"A perfectly reasonable explanation," Alice said, and patted Liam's shoulder. "You'll take care of them, then?"

"I'll put them in my garden," he said, still staring at his wrist. He held it out to her. "That wasn't a turtle."

Alice looked at the faint but neat semicircle of toothmarks on his wrist, and reflected that it had been considerate of the dryads not to set the turtles on him immediately. "The dog did bite you too, dear."

"Not until later."

She regarded him levelly. "Are you saying something *else* bit you, as well as the turtle and the dog? Something *else* was hiding in the tree? That seems like a stretch."

"Well, I mean, maybe, but—"

"There we are, then." She looked at Jasmine. "Our tea's going to be quite cold."

"It will," Jasmine said, and added to Liam, "I am sorry about Primrose."

"Sure," he said, and sighed. "Do we have to finish the tree?"

"Yes," Si said, not sounding particularly enthusiastic. "But there shouldn't be any more turtles, right?"

"I'm sure that's all of them," Alice said. "I think you'll be absolutely fine now." And she led the way back to the bakery, picking their way through the Christmas shoppers. She waited until they were settled at their table again, a new pot of tea ordered, before she said, "Are you alright, Jasmine?"

"It was only a nip," Jasmine said, inspecting the dressing on her arm. "She didn't mean it."

"Of course she didn't," Alice said, and gave the dog a narrow look. Primrose bared her teeth.

"She was very brave and terribly clever," Jasmine added,

picking the dog up and kissing the top of her head while she wriggled and growled.

"Of course she was," Alice said, and cut her cupcake in half, spilling dark crumbs onto the plate. Outside, the Toot Hansell Christmas tree slowly rose over the warm, dancing lights of the square, and two snapping turtles paced grumpily in the back of a council truck, thoroughly annoyed at having been removed from a quite nicely muddy tarn and randomly thrown at people. It was not, they felt, either dignified or in the Christmas spirit.

They intended to express their displeasure at the earliest opportunity, and as sharply as possible.

CHRISTMAS PUDDING CUPCAKES

For someone with a substantially sweet tooth, I'm weirdly ambivalent about cupcakes. So many of them seem to exist as merely a vehicle for icing. And while I make no objections to icing (it is, after all, delightful), I still feel that anything with "cake" in its name should hold up its end of the bargain. Which means having a delightful and delicious and – I'm sorry, I have to say it – *moist* cake under all that icing. Otherwise it should just call itself a cup-icing. Icing-cup?

Now, I first made these because they're ridiculously cute, and that seemed worth suffering a less than perfect cake for. But, of course, the cake is terribly important because the icing is merely decoration, not 80% of the cupcake's reason for existence. So the first version was merely "eh." All style, no substance, as the bakers are regularly accused of on *Bake Off*.

But because they are so cute, I decided there had to be a way to make the eating as delightful as the seeing. Which there is.

And I'm currently deciding how I can repurpose the mix for all other occasions, because it's that tasty. And *moist*.

Sorry.

For the cupcakes:

- 95 g / ¾ cup flour
- 45 g / a bit less than ½ cup cocoa
- ¾ tsp baking powder
- ½ tsp baking soda
- ¼ tsp salt
- 2 eggs
- 200 g / 1 cup sugar
- 80 mL / ⅓ cup vegetable oil
- 120 mL / ½ cup yoghurt – I used raspberry because I had it, but plain or cherry would be lovely
- 100 g / ⅔ cup chopped sour cherries

For the icing:

- 75 g / ¾ cup icing sugar

Preheat oven to 180°C / 350°F. Butter a 12-hole muffin tin – you *can* use cupcake liners, but we're going to be decorating the bottoms, so you'll have to peel them off anyway. I found a good layer of butter and the gentle use of a knife to help them out worked just fine.

Sift or whisk together the flour, cocoa, baking powder, baking soda, and salt.

In a separate bowl lightly whisk together the eggs, sugar, and oil. Add the dry ingredients and stir to *just* combine (it's going to be a runny mix). Gently fold in the cherries.

Fill the muffin tin to about halfway on each hole – we want flat tops, so not too much in each. You'll have some left over, so you can make a second batch of anywhere between 2 and 4 more, depending on the size of your pan.

Bake about 20 minutes, checking at around 18 to see how they're doing. Cool in the tray for about 10 minutes before carefully removing them.

Once your cupcakes are completely cool, combine your icing sugar with a teeny bit of water (or you could use orange juice, or even cherry liqueur if you wanted to be fancy), adding it bit by bit until you have an icing that's runny enough to make your drips on the side of the cakes, but thick enough that it won't just all run off. Turn your cupcakes bottoms-up, and scoop a heaped teaspoon of icing onto the new top. Work the back of the teaspoon in gentle circles over the icing, encouraging it to spread out and run down the side here and there. You should end up with the sort of white topping you see in pictures of classic Christmas pudding, spilling a little down the sides but still showing the dark cake for the most part. Top with sugarcraft holly for instant fanciness (of course I bought them. Making sugarcraft holly is not on my list of Things To Do).

Done! Makes 16-ish, but I actually get 12 nicely sized ones (to my mind) from a half batch. You can freeze them before icing, if you want.

3

THREE FRENCH HENS

Martha wandered up to Pearl with a daisy-print welly in her mouth, and offered it to her.

Pearl took the welly gravely, and gave the old Labrador a good scratch around the ears. "Thank you, dear," she said.

Martha grunted and looked at her hopefully.

"You have just had breakfast," Pearl said, but gave her a biscuit from her coat pocket anyway. Martha crunched it down, then looked expectant.

"I don't think so." Pearl turned to lead the way up the long, thin wedge of her back garden. It wasn't even light yet, and it was already their second trip out into the sharp-edged morning, frost reflecting early light on the rooftops and shrubs transformed into abstract, glittering sculptures. Porridge, she thought. Such a morning called for porridge.

She opened the kitchen door onto a flood of warmth and mellow gold light, kicking her shoes off on the mat and waving the welly at Martha.

"Do come on, dear. All the warmth is getting out."

Martha broke into a shamble that bore a distant resemblance to a jog, and Pearl peered into the welly. Something had moved in it when she'd waved it at Martha. It was probably a stone. The old Labrador adored them, for some reason, and more than once Pearl had been forced to carry some mud-encrusted, lichen-covered miniature boulder back from a walk because Martha howled piteously if she had to leave it behind. She looked up as Martha arrived at the doorway, the dog's soft brown eyes gently coated with cataracts.

"Well," she said, sticking her hand in the boot and finding something smooth and symmetrical. "It's called eccentricity at our age, isn't it?" Martha wagged her tail in agreement, and Pearl fished out what looked an awful lot like a slightly chubbier than usual egg. She blinked at it. Chubby, and also … "Is that purple?" she asked Martha.

"I'd call it more violet," a new voice said from the garden, making Pearl jump, and Teresa leaned into the kitchen. She was wearing her dressing gown and a woolly hat. "Shall I put the kettle on?"

"Yes," Pearl said, still staring at the egg. Teresa stepped onto the kitchen mat and plucked the egg out of her hand to examine it.

"How odd. Does it feel a bit warm?"

"I just thought my hands were cold."

Teresa tucked the egg into her dressing gown pocket and took one of Pearl's hands in both of hers. "They are. Come and warm up."

"Just a moment." Pearl investigated the boot. "Look, there's another." She handed it over, the same soft, almost pastel purple as the first, but maybe a tiny bit bigger.

"It's the wrong time of year for these," Teresa said, as Pearl found a third egg. "I've never heard of Christmas eggs."

"And one would expect more tinsel and glitter," Pearl said, putting the boot on the rack and checking the other shoes. "Plus maybe a different colour scheme. That seems to be all of them, though."

"Enough for an omelette," Teresa said.

"We're not *eating* them," Pearl said. "Can anything that colour really be edible? And how old are they?"

Teresa shook one next to her ear. "It sounds alright."

"Tell you that, did it?"

They both laughed, and Teresa scuffed out of her trainers and went to put the kettle on, her Christmas penguin leggings bright under her dressing gown.

THE DAY RAN AWAY on Pearl, what with a Women's Institute meeting to finalise plans for the Christmas market stall, and last-minute shopping for what she needed to make, and a quick visit to the vet to check Martha's ears (she was no deafer than before, the vet declared. Just more stubborn). It seemed the sky had barely lightened before it was dark again, and she was staring at the contents of her over-full fridge, wondering how she had so much food when it was just her and Martha and sometimes Teresa. A cold wet nose found her hand, and she looked down.

"You've already eaten," Pearl said, and Martha wagged her tail in a manner that suggested she'd either already forgotten, or was very open to the idea of seconds. Pearl looked back at the fridge, then sighed, shut it, and opened the freezer compartment instead. She fished out a Tupperware of little homity pies, all crisp pastry shells and silky spinach and a comforting amount of potatoes and cheese.

"That'll do," she said, and carried them out the back door and down the garden path, Martha plodding amiably along behind her. She went through the gate that connected her garden with the one of the next house in the terraced row, up the path, and let them both in the back door, setting the wind chimes by the window dinging softly.

Teresa looked up from the paper as Pearl padded into the kitchen. "Hello, dear. Hello, Martha." Martha ambled over to see if there was food on offer, then slumped to the floor in front of the oven with a sigh.

Pearl sat down opposite Teresa at the tiny, two-person table and said, "Are you sure we shouldn't just knock through the wall? It's cold out."

"We've had twenty years of not knocking through," Teresa said, folding the paper. "Besides, what would the neighbours say?"

Pearl snorted. "As if that's ever bothered you."

"It'd be expensive."

"Not between two of us."

"Fine," Teresa said, folding her arms over her slim chest. "You snore when you have wine with dinner. I can hear it even *with* the wall."

They stared at each other for a moment, then Pearl laughed and Teresa grinned, and Martha's tail thumped the floor softly, her unfocused gaze moving between them.

"Homity pies for dinner?" Pearl asked.

"Lovely. I'll make salad."

"Perfect. Just not so many chillies in the dressing this time. I couldn't taste my tea for two days after that last one."

"There was barely any in there!"

"There was a whole chilli bush in there."

"Rubbish," Teresa said.

They ate in the living room, sitting on the sofa with their plates balanced on their knees, watching *Death in Paradise* and turning the volume up over Martha's snores. The wood burner rumbled in the hearth and the lights of the Christmas tree were reflected in the uncurtained windows like mysterious, friendly constellations, winking at the dark and promising magic.

IT HAD STARTED RAINING by the time Pearl went home, hurrying down the path to the gate and feeling harsh edges in the night that suggested the rain was on the verge of turning to sleet. The heating would have gone off at home by now, and the idea of her small dark house was suddenly so far from the cosiness of Teresa's living room that she considered going back. But Teresa got up at a completely uncivilised hour to do her exercises, and Pearl was a morning person only as required by Martha. So she tucked her fleece a little closer around her and trotted up her own path, calling to the Labrador to hurry up, as much as that was possible.

The kitchen still smelled faintly of the chutney she'd made the day before, a warm, spicy scent, and she'd forgotten to leave a light on. She leaned in the door, fumbling for the light switch on the wall while she tried not to step in with her mucky boots, then stopped.

There was a ... not a light, exactly. A *glow*. A pale, cold illumination swelling and fading like the beat of a heart, painting the walls in chilly colour. Pearl blinked at it. It wasn't the oven, or the fridge, or anything else she could think of. She'd never seen anything like it before. Martha whined next to her, and she patted the old dog's head lightly. "It's okay," she said, abandoning the light switch and pulling her boots off. "Nothing to worry about."

Martha whined, apparently not reassured, and Pearl crept into the oddly unfamiliar kitchen in her socks, hoping she wasn't going to have to run anywhere. The glow was coming from the little table, where the fruit bowl sat. For a brief, confused moment she wondered if she'd accidentally bought some strange new breed of festive apples, like those glow-in-the-dark fish. Not that she'd ever heard of glow-in-the-dark *apples*, but there were always new varieties coming out. Or maybe some sort of radioactive spider had come in with the bananas. She *had* heard of those.

Well, plain spiders, not radioactive ones. But there was always a first.

She peered into the fruit bowl, ready to jump back if a genetically unexpected spider leaped out at her, and said, "Oh."

There were no glowing fruit, no radioactive spiders. Just the eggs, where Teresa must have left them, pulsing with that pale, near-violet light, and every time it brightened, the shells were rendered almost translucent. Inside each of them she could see something coiled tightly, all scales and claws and patience.

"Oh," she said again, and looked at Martha. "Not Christmas bunny eggs, then."

Martha just wagged her tail and looked at the treats tin. Some things were more important than glowing, inhabited eggs.

THE THING about dragons is that they're not that easy to get in touch with. One can't just drop them a text, or send them a Facebook message. Not even the most modern of dragons have mobile phones – or certainly not the dragons they knew. So it was three days later when Pearl, Teresa, Miriam and Mortimer stood in Pearl's kitchen, staring at the eggs. They were still in the fruit bowl, although Pearl had taken all the other fruit out and, after some thought, had thrown it in the fire rather than in the compost. Just in case. She'd also lined the bowl with an old, soft jumper, so the eggs were cradled in a deep pink nest.

Mortimer put his heavy front paws on the table and peered at the eggs. He was still mostly his own lovely deep purple-blue, but there was some anxious grey colouring creeping around his snout.

"Do you know what they are?" Pearl asked.

"Umm," he said, and nudged an egg gently. "Well. I mean, *eggs*, obviously. Magic ones."

"We did rather gather that from the glowing," Teresa said. "It was a bit of a giveaway."

"Right," Mortimer said, the grey spreading. "Of course."

"Homity pie?" Pearl asked, offering Mortimer a plate.

"*Ooh,*" he said, abandoning the eggs. "What's a homity?"

There was a moment of silence as the three women looked at each other.

"Potatoes?" Miriam ventured.

"Homity potatoes?" Pearl said doubtfully. "I've not heard of those."

"Maybe it's an old strain that's died out," Teresa suggested.

They considered it, then Pearl shook her head. "Never mind that. What about the eggs? What am I supposed to do with them?"

Mortimer, his mouth full of pie and another already in his paw, swallowed hurriedly. "I don't know," he admitted. "I'll have to ask Beaufort. Maybe you should put them outside for now. You know, just in case."

"Just in case of what?" Teresa asked.

"Well, anything can hatch out of an egg," Mortimer said, and popped the second pie in his mouth.

"Like alligators," Miriam said, twisting her hands together and staring at the eggs. "Or dinosaurs."

"They're extinct," Pearl said. "There's hardly been a Stegosaurus laying eggs in my wellies."

"Well, they're not chicken eggs, are they?" Teresa said. "Not with the glowing."

"May I have another of those?" Mortimer asked, eyeing the plate. "I think I rather like homity."

ONCE YOU *HAVE* CONTACTED A DRAGON, of course, it's much easier to contact other dragons. Which is why, as the night dropped heavy skirts over a Toot Hansell awash in Christmas lights and low smoke drifting from old chimneys, Pearl opened the door to Mortimer and Beaufort Scales, High Lord of the Cloverly dragons, who was currently sporting a flat tweed cap.

"Hello, you two," she said. "Nice hat, Beaufort."

"Thank you," he said. "I understand many detectives favour distinctive modes of dress, so I thought I'd try a cap. Not much good for flying, though."

"I can see that being an issue," Pearl said, stepping back to let them in. "Have you tried some elastic to hold it on?"

"I was wondering about a scarf," Beaufort said. "Elastic seems a little undignified."

"Quite," Pearl said. "Anyway, thank you for being so quick."

"This is most interesting," Beaufort said. "And I wasn't busy."

"You were meant to be busy," Mortimer said as Pearl closed the night out behind them. "You were meant to be settling that dispute between the High Fells wyrms and the Barking dragons, before they start trying to set landslides on each other again."

Beaufort waved a paw dismissively. "It's been going on forever. It doesn't matter how often I mediate, they'll be back again in a few decades. *This*, however …" He grinned at Pearl, exposing an impressive array of yellowed teeth. "Unidentified eggs! How exciting."

"She won't put them outside," Teresa said, peering into the kitchen from the living room. "She says they might get cold."

"Well, it's very chilly out," Pearl said. "And damp."

"Alligators," Teresa reminded her. "Dinosaurs!"

"Pearl's right, though," Miriam said, leaning around Teresa. "Yorkshire isn't exactly known for its alligators."

"Well, not *literal* alligators and dinosaurs," Teresa said.

"I didn't realise there were any other sort," Beaufort said, sitting back on his haunches and looking around the kitchen. "Where are these pesky eggs, then?"

"I put them by the hearth to warm them up," Pearl said, and Teresa made a noise that was the vocal equivalent of an eye-roll. Pearl frowned at her. "What if they're an endangered species? We don't know!"

"They might make *us* an endangered species," Teresa said. "When has any good come from unidentified eggs?"

"I hatched ducks once," Miriam said. "Well, ducklings, I mean. From shop eggs. They were very sweet."

"Yes, but you *expected* ducklings," Teresa pointed out. "These are glow-in-the-dark eggs. They could be aliens, for all we know."

Pearl ignored them and looked at Beaufort, who was watching the exchange with enormous interest, his old gold eyes reflecting the warm light of the kitchen. "Tea?" she offered. "And Miriam brought some mince pies."

"Yes, please," Mortimer said immediately. "You wouldn't have any cream, by any chance?"

"No," Pearl said. "But I've got some Wensleydale cheese."

"*Ooh,*" the High Lord said, and grinned.

PEARL'S little living room felt even smaller when occupied by three women and two not enormous but not insubstantial dragons, all of them gathered in a semicircle around the hearth. Martha snored on the rug directly in front of the fire, and only twitched when she caught a whiff of the cheese. The eggs snuggled in their blanket on a small table just to the side of the hearth, and Beaufort leaned over them, examining them without touching them.

"Glow in the dark, you say?"

"More like pulsing," Teresa said. "Like an infection."

"It's very pretty," Pearl protested. "You watch too many of those awful movies."

"I like those movies," Teresa said. "And I'm far better prepared for pulsing eggs because of them."

"I don't know how anyone can really be prepared for pulsing eggs," Miriam said. Martha looked up to make sure no one had dropped any cheese, sighed, and closed her eyes again.

"Would you please stop saying pulsing?" Pearl asked. "Do you know what they are, Beaufort?"

The High Lord of the Cloverly dragons sat back on his haunches with his front paws pressed over his broad chest, gave a thoughtful *hmm*, released a stream of green smoke from his nostrils, and said, "Not a clue."

"Oh," Pearl, Teresa and Miriam said.

"Would anyone mind if I had another mince pie?" Mortimer asked.

"Of course not, Mortimer. Help yourself," Pearl said, then turned back to Beaufort. "So no idea what they were doing in my welly, then?"

Beaufort leaned forward and tapped one of the eggs gently. "Some creatures don't nest as such. They just leave their eggs in a safe spot and trust the world to sort things out. Sometimes it even works."

"Some creatures? What sort of creatures?" Miriam asked.

"Poisonous ones?" Teresa suggested. "Extraterrestrial ones?"

"Oh, all sorts," Beaufort said. "Knuckers. Gargoyles – although they're usually stone and left in chimneys. Faeries."

"Faeries lay eggs?" Pearl asked. "I never imagined that."

"You don't want a clutch of those in your garden," Mortimer said, taking a large slurp of tea. "The mess!"

Pearl opened her mouth to ask what sort of mess, exactly, and was interrupted by a *tap* from the table. They turned to look, and one of the eggs gave a little shudder and a soft surge of light that was visible even in the warmly lit room.

"Well, now," Beaufort said, and tapped the egg in reply.

Tap, came immediately from inside, and it bounced a little on the spot. One of the others gave a sharp little glow, and the third shivered. The glow wasn't making them as translucent as the night before, but Pearl could still see changing shades inside, like the creature was moving about rapidly.

"I don't think they're faeries," she said. "They looked scaly."

Beaufort looked at her. "You saw them?"

"Through the shell. They were all curled up, but I could see scales and claws."

"That sounds promising," Teresa said.

Beaufort scooped the eggs out of the bowl, cradling them on the heavy pads of his paws. "There are two possibilities with eggs, of course. One is that they imprint on the first thing they see. The other is that they ... well, don't."

"Oh no," Mortimer said. He was clutching his mug in both paws. "You're not thinking of peatniks?"

"Peatniks?" Miriam demanded. "What on earth are they?"

Pearl had sudden visions of small dragons wearing berets and quoting Ginsberg emerging from the eggs, and Beaufort said, "A variety of sprite. They live in peat bogs and are very solitary creatures. They ... well, the first to hatch eats the others."

"Ew," Pearl and Miriam said.

"Fantastic," Teresa said.

"Not much to eat in peat bogs for a very young sprite," Beaufort said. "They can't be stealing sheep as soon as they hatch."

"Well, maybe we should put them outside," Miriam said. "Just in case."

"Yes," Teresa said. "Sensible."

"It's just ... there's going to be a frost," Pearl pointed out. "And there's no peat to keep them warm."

"Oh, I don't actually think they're peatniks," Beaufort said. "I don't recognise the eggs at all. I'm just saying that these sorts of things do happen with some eggs."

"We're not putting them outside," Pearl said. "I rather feel they've been given to me for safekeeping. They *were* left in my welly."

Teresa starting saying something about aliens, and Miriam talked over her, asking what about the imprinting problem, and Pearl said she wasn't going to listen to either of them, because the egg had been in *her* boot, and Beaufort put the eggs down on the hearth and took a mince pie from Mortimer. And the discussion looked set to go on for quite some time, until someone shouted, *"Merde!"*

"Excuse me?" Teresa said, and they turned to look at the hearth. A small lizard stood in the wreckage of one of the eggs, hugging its two front legs around its chest and standing on four others, skinny tail whipping like an angry cat's. It was a lovely silvery grey and stared at them with bulging violet eyes.

"Putain!" it screamed. *"Il fait froid!"*

"Interesting," Beaufort said.

"Où est le soleil, connard? Où?"

"They're French," Mortimer said. "How are they French?"

"Maybe they were on holiday," Beaufort suggested.

"In my welly?" Pearl asked.

The lizard stopped hugging itself and waved rather rudely, still shouting.

"They seem very upset," Miriam said. "Can anyone speak French?"

"I'm not translating all of it," Teresa said. "They're very rude. But they're cold and angry about it, basically."

One of the remaining eggs gave a shudder and a sudden, brilliant pulse of colour, then the shell shattered. A second lizard unrolled itself, lunging to its feet and shaking itself off. *"Putain!"* it shrieked. *"Qu'est-ce tu fait? Merde!"*

The first lizard turned to look at the newcomer, and pointed at Beaufort. *"C'est lui! C'est de sa faute! Connard!"*

"*Connard!*" the second one agreed, so loudly that Martha lumbered to her feet and retreated into the kitchen.

"I think imprinting is out," Teresa observed, as the third egg shattered and the last of the lizards leaped to its feet. "They're very upset and think it's all our fault. Well, Beaufort's, particularly."

"I say," Beaufort said. "That's a bit unfair."

"*Où est-ce?*" the third lizard demanded. "*Pourquoi est-il si froid?*"

"*Les anglais,*" the first one said, waving at the room.

"*LES ANGLAIS?*" the other two gasped.

"Oh dear," Beaufort said. "That's us, isn't it? The English?"

"*Je déteste les anglais,*" the third lizard announced, setting off a chorus of shouting that Pearl couldn't understand but rather got the gist of anyway.

"That's a bit unnecessary, whatever it is," Miriam said.

Beaufort patted the hearth with one heavy paw. "That's quite enough. You're guests."

The second lizard put his hands on his hips. "*Rosbif,*" he declared, and the other two cheered.

"What?" Mortimer asked.

"He just called us roast beef," Teresa said. "It's a traditional insult."

Beaufort lowered his head and growled, a rumbling sound that Pearl could feel in her feet, and all three lizards shrieked, falling over each other as they spun around and shot up the chimney.

"*Putain!*" one screeched from a safe distance, and then there was silence, just a little soot falling into the open fire.

"Are they gone?" Miriam asked, and a few shouted insults came from the chimney.

"Are they *staying?*" Teresa asked. "What if they grow?"

"What do they eat?" Pearl asked, and they all looked at Beaufort.

"Ah," he said, scratching an ear. "Well. We determined they were French, of course. And magical. Also a bit rude."

"You still don't know what they are, do you?" Teresa asked.

"No," the High Lord admitted.

"Wonderful," Pearl said. "So I've got unidentified French lizards living in my chimney now?"

"Rude ones," Miriam said, as a small *merde* drifted from the fireplace.

"I did tell you to leave them outside," Teresa said, and Pearl glared at her. "Oh, don't. You can set them on carol singers."

"I *like* carol singers."

"You do not. You wanted to throw eggnog on that one last year."

"He was terrible."

"Well, now you can set rude French lizards on him," Teresa said, and grinned.

"That hardly seems in the Christmas spirit," Miriam observed, and lifted her hands as both women turned toward her. "I just mean that eggnog is more festive."

"What's that about eggnog?" Beaufort asked. He'd been peering up the chimney, and had soot on his snout. His scales were glowing with the heat of the fire, and his hat had started smouldering. Teresa grabbed it and patted it out. "Did someone say there was eggnog?"

"Umm. I've got more tea?" Pearl offered.

"Oh," Beaufort said. "Well, that'll be lovely too."

Teresa patted his shoulder. "Do you know, I think I've got some next door. Bought stuff, but it's rather good."

"Bought?" Pearl said. "How could you?"

Teresa stuck her tongue out and headed for the kitchen, legs long in Christmas pudding-print leggings. Pearl and Miriam looked at each other.

"Maybe the smoke will drive them out?" Miriam suggested.

"I don't want to burn them alive," Pearl said. She knelt on the hearth, trying to peer up the chimney without getting too close to the fire. A large lump of soot crashed down, disrupting the logs and scattering black dust everywhere. "Stop that!"

"You won't need a chimney cleaner, anyway. You can just shout at them and they'll do it all."

"Silver linings and all that," Pearl said, and got up, looking at the dragons. "Do we need more mince pies to go with the eggnog?"

"It'd be rude to turn them down," Beaufort said, grinning. Pearl smiled at him and went into the kitchen to find some glasses and more mince pies, thinking that three French lizards in one's chimney was unfortunate, but still better than exploding baubles or magical snow monsters roaming the village. One had to look on the bright side.

She just hoped they didn't grow too much.

HOMITY PIES

Homity pies are just the best comfort food. I'd only had them a couple of times before my lovely editor and her friend came to visit, at which point I decided (as I usually do) that since I had guests, I should cook something I'd never cooked before. Ahem.

And it really is a perfect pie for entertaining. It's lovely hot, but still tasty cold, it freezes and reheats well, and it just shouts, "Look at me being all comfort-food-y and adorable!" I can't think of anything better to have on hand for after days out with friends, or for an easy holiday meal, or in case of dragons.

It also lends itself to all sorts of pastry. I've made it with whole-meal shortcrust pastry that complimented the flavours beautifully and could be pressed thinly into the tin. It'd be amazing with filo pastry, too, which would lend a lovely crunch on the edges. When we made little party pies, though, that could easily be made ahead and frozen, the SO went for a raised pie pastry that's nice and robust and isn't going to fall to pieces on the first bite. But I'd just use whatever you have on hand, to be honest.

Just don't tell the SO I said that. He won't help me come up with recipes anymore if I keep messing with them ...

For the pastry:

- 500 g / 4 cups flour
- 20 g / 1 Tbsp salt
- 200 g / 10 Tbsp / 4 oz butter
- 5 egg yolks mixed with 125 mL / ½ cup water

Combine flour and salt, then rub the butter in until completely combined. Make a well in the centre and pour the egg yolk mix into it, then work it slowly into the flour. Knead just until combined, then pop it in the fridge for about half an hour.

Roll out to a thickness of about 3 mm / 0.1 inch, then cut to fit your muffin tin / mini pie tray. Press gently into the tray (if using a muffin tin you only want it to go around 3/4 of the way up), then return to the fridge until you're ready to fill them. (This is going to make far more than you need, but you can wrap the remaining dough in clingfilm and freeze it until you make another batch.)

For the pies:

- 850 g / a bit less than 2 lbs potatoes, peeled and diced into small-ish chunks
- 25 g / just under 2 Tbsp / just under 1 oz butter
- 1 Tbsp oil
- 3 diced onions – if you have leeks, about 3 of them (white parts only) plus a red onion are lovely
- 2 cloves finely chopped / minced garlic
- 100 g / 3 ½ cups / 3 ½ oz fresh spinach (or use frozen and measure by weight)
- 175 g / 1 ¾ cups / 6 oz-ish grated cheese (I always like strong cheddar for flavour, but you could use any cheese you fancy here)

- 250 mL / 1 cup cream
- Herbs to taste – thyme is nice!
- Salt and pepper to taste
- Mustard if wanted – I used around a Tbsp of wholegrain

Preheat the oven to 200°C/ just under 400°F.

Cook the potatoes until just tender. Drain.

Melt the butter and oil in a frying pan and fry the onions gently until soft and pale golden-brown. Add the garlic and your herbs of choice, then cook for a couple more minutes, stirring regularly.

Combine the onion mix with the potatoes, then mix with about half the cheese, the spinach, mustard and seasoning.

Spoon into the pastry cases, then pour the cream over the top, making sure you spread it as equally as possible so it can trickle down through the layers. Top with the remaining cheese.

Cover the tray with a sheet of foil and bake for 20 minutes, then remove the foil and give it another 10.

Eat hot or cold!

Makes 12 lovely little party pies, but if you want to make one big pie, just use the same filling. Line a big springform pan with your pastry, and bake for about 45 minutes, setting the pan on a roasting tray in case of leaks. It'll feed about 8.

4

FOUR CALLING BIRDS

"Who's a clever boy, then?" Carlotta asked, scratching the parrot's head. "Who's the best birdie in the whole wide world?"

"Bertie is," the parrot croaked, eyes drifting closed in pleasure. "Bertie's a clever boy."

"Yes he *is*," Carlotta said, and gave him a slice of carrot. "There you go. Eat up!" She turned back to the kitchen, separated from the rest of the big living and dining room by a squat island covered with drifts of icing sugar and almond crumbs.

Bertie looked at the piece of carrot, then at the ranks of amaretti biscuits lined up on the island, and said in a rather lower voice, "Bollocks."

Carlotta turned back, frowning. "What was that?"

"Bertie want a biscuit," the parrot said.

"Oh, you *are* clever. No biscuits for Bertie, though. Too much sugar for birdies." She started stacking the biscuits in tins, and the parrot sighed.

He nibbled the carrot without much enthusiasm for a bit, then straightened up and shouted, "Show us what you got!"

Carlotta flapped a tea towel at him. "You just behave yourself!"

He gave a low whistle, dancing on his perch. "Gizza kiss! Show us your baps!"

"Bloody hell, Carly," Philip said, wandering in with his hands in his pockets. "Is that bird ever going to shut up?"

"I don't know," she said, slapping his hand away as he reached for an amaretti and picking a different one to offer him instead. "But your language isn't helping. And I think he's still settling in."

"If you say so," he said, taking the biscuit and looking from it to the one he'd reached for. "What's the difference?"

"That one's a funny shape."

He stared at it. "It is?"

"Work it, baby!" the parrot squawked, and dropped his carrot.

Philip and Carlotta looked at him. "Where did Toni get him again?" Philip asked.

"He was a rescue."

Bertie wolf-whistled and bobbed his head.

"From where – a strip club?"

Carlotta slapped his shoulder lightly. "He belonged to someone in Leeds, and apparently he was fine until they started building next to her. She used to let him sit on the porch, and the next thing she knew he'd picked up all these expressions from the builders. She'd have kept him, but she runs a day care, so it was bit inappropriate."

"Kids probably loved it," Philip said.

"Ooo-er," Bertie added.

Philip took a bite of the amaretti, scattering icing sugar all over his jumper. "So why do we have him?"

"Toni couldn't keep him," Carlotta said. "Not with Emily. Imagine our granddaughter's first word being bollocks."

"Or baps," Philip said, and she poked him in the side. "What? He could've just been asking for a salad roll!"

"Behave," she said, glancing at the clock. "I've got to go. Don't eat any of the good biscuits!"

"I don't know how you tell the difference," he said, inspecting the ranks of sweet-smelling amaretti on the cooling rack, but she was already hurrying out of the room. He selected one at random.

"Tap that booty," Bertie observed.

Philip looked at him for a moment, checked Carlotta hadn't come back downstairs, and took a biscuit to the bird. "In honour of an impressive vocabulary," he said, as the parrot took the offering delicately in his beak.

Bertie swapped the biscuit to his claw. "Thanks, mate," he said.

Philip stared at him. "What?"

The parrot squawked, and turned his attention to the amaretti. Philip watched him for a moment, then went to put the kettle on. Smart birds, parrots. Not smart enough to actually have a conversation with, though. He didn't think, anyway. He peered out the window over the sink as he waited for the kettle to boil. Three crows were huddled on the bird feeder, shoulders hunched against a fine rain, staring at Bertie. Now, there were some other smart birds. Not as mouthy though, which was probably a good thing.

"Bollocks," Bertie said, as the biscuit broke and fell to the floor. "Bertie wants his biscuit."

Philip sighed and went to pick it up.

GILBERT CREPT THROUGH THE GARDEN, his scales flushed the muted greens and browns of the winter foliage, such as it was. He hadn't quite anticipated that the gardens would be *so* bare, and he was worried he might be leaving some very obvious footprints, despite having fashioned tactical socks out of old scales. These left tracks that, when looked at from the right angle in low light (and if one ignored the tail track running between them, and was feeling imaginative), somewhat resembled hoof prints. Maybe. If the horse in question had a rather unusual gait and was slightly pigeon-toed.

He settled himself under the cover of a hedge, watching the bird through the window. It was a little drab, but most unusual, and he was fairly certain that it wasn't an English bird, which meant it was not only imprisoned inside, but had been kidnapped from its own country. He couldn't just ignore that. He'd promised Mortimer there'd be no more turkey liberation operations this year (Amelia kept calling it stealing, but she was both *such* a tool of the establishment and his sister, so that was only to be expected), but no one had said anything about freeing foreign avian prisoners. For one moment he thought of Mortimer's shedding tail, and how it tended to get worse when any sort of even mildly revolutionary work was involved, then he pushed the thought away. No. He couldn't let the risk of Mortimer's bald patch stop him. This bird needed to be *free.*

And he'd ask Miriam for some more coconut oil for Mortimer's tail. That would make up for it, anyway.

THE MAN in the plaid jumper spent forever in the same room as the bird, making tea and a large ham and cheese sandwich (Gilbert's stomach growled at the idea of cheese, but he ignored it. Such were the privations of a freedom fighter). He ate sitting in a large easy chair with his back to the bird while it puttered from one end of its perch to the other, obviously languishing in boredom and despair. The man watched TV and ate terribly slowly, and before long Gilbert was languishing a little himself. There wasn't even anything very interesting on the TV that he could see – just a lot of people shouting at each other, and bigger people holding them back now and then when they got too excited. He wondered if there were any more birds in the neighbouring houses he could liberate first, then come back to this one. Or maybe some rabbits being held against their will.

He was almost ready to go and investigate, even though he'd reconnoitred the whole street before deciding the parrot was his primary target (there were some hamsters in a cage a couple of doors over, but they were quite small and the cage was quite big, so he wasn't sure they really needed rescuing. Plus, the odds of Walter thinking they were afternoon tea were quite high if he took them back to the caverns). But just before he gave up his vigil the man finally got up, switching the TV off. He washed his plate and mug, then wandered out of sight, returned with a heavy jacket on, vanished again, and finally Gilbert heard the slam of the front door.

This was it. He scuttled forward, belly low to the ground, his flanks smeared with mud and stripes daubed across his face. He'd even painted his talons green and brown, and taken his tail piercings out in case the glint of light on them gave him away. He skirted a flower bed, took a quick look around, and dashed across the paved patio to the doors.

The parrot was looking at him with interest, and he waved, trying to smile without showing any teeth. Far too many of those he liberated assumed he was going to eat them, and he would *never*. He was a vegetarian, as befitted a defender of the equality of all creatures. The parrot lifted a foot in return, so that was something. It complicated the rescue efforts when they panicked and started running about the place screeching. He glanced around again, got up on his haunches, and took some tools from a band around his foreleg. He'd had a particularly helpful dwarf make them up, and it was the work of a moment to open the lock. Magical lock picks worked even better than the regular ones they were modelled on.

"Hey," he said to the parrot. "Don't be scared. I'm Gilbert. I'm here to set you free."

"What?" the parrot said, startling him. The chickens never talked back.

"You talk," he said.

"So do you," the parrot said. "What are you, anyway? Some sort of iguana?"

"Okay," Gilbert said, wondering how this changed things. He'd never had to explain the situation before. "Sure. This is cool. Totally cool."

"Shut the door," the parrot said. "It's cold out."

"Um," Gilbert looked out at the garden. "I'm going to rescue you. So the door kind of needs to be open for our getaway."

"Bollocks to that," the parrot said. "That's my door. Shut the damn thing."

"Look – what's your name?"

"Bertie."

"Okay. Bertie, you're being held against your will," Gilbert said. "And I think you may have developed Stockport syndrome." That wasn't quite right, but he knew what he meant.

"Stock-what?"

"Stock ... pot syndrome?" No, that wasn't it either. "Look, you're sympathising with your captors and now *want* to stay, only you wouldn't if you were thinking straight."

"Well, you can get right off," Bertie said, only it wasn't *quite* what he said. Gilbert didn't recognise the word he used, but he thought it probably wasn't suitable for young dragons who weren't even in their sixties yet. "Go on. And shut the bloody door behind you, you scaly little git."

"But I'm liberating you! I'm the resistance! A lone warrior railing against the terrible forces who would imprison you, howling for the freedom of all—"

"You're letting the cold in!" Bertie bawled, and Gilbert jumped, stumbling onto the clean, pale wood floor in his muddy hoof-socks.

"Oh no," he said, looking down.

"Git," the parrot said, then suddenly straightened up. "Shut the door! Quick, shut the damn door!"

"I won't let you accept your captivity! I can free you!" Gilbert shouted, and scampered toward the parrot's perch to cut the little leash on his foot.

"Shut the door!" Bertie shrieked, and from outside came the sudden thunder of a feathered invasion. Gilbert spun around, but the crows were already inside, sweeping past the dragon and the parrot to descend on the trays and tins of biscuits, shrieking in delight. *"Get out!"* Bertie shouted at them.

"Sod off," one of the crows shouted back.

"Bollocks!" a second one jeered, and the third chortled, its beak already full of biscuit.

Bertie glared at Gilbert. "Look what you've done, you complete numpty!"

"Oh, no," Gilbert whispered. "This is even worse than the turkeys."

"Get them *out*," Bertie insisted.

"Right," Gilbert said, and approached the crows. Icing sugar hung in a cloud around the kitchen island, accompanied by a few feathers. He was still trailing mud everywhere, but that seemed rather less important than it had a moment ago. "Right, you lot," he said, trying to sound authoritative. "You have to leave. You can't be in here."

The biggest crow looked at him, put its head on one side, and said, "Crow wants a biscuit."

Gilbert stared at him, then at Bertie, who said something that was definitely unrepeatable. Gilbert had never actually been spoken to by a bird before, and now there were four of them, and they were all kind of rude. This was getting weird.

"Gizza kiss!" one of the other crows shouted, inexplicably, and the rest of them cawed raucously. Gilbert had the uncomfortable (and, he was fairly sure, accurate) feeling that they were laughing at him.

"You have to leave!" he shouted at them. "This is a rescue mission for a captured foreign avian, and you're *ruining* it!"

The crows stopped cawing and just stared at him, which was actually no improvement. "You what?" one said.

"You're going to ruin the mission," he said, feeling his camouflaged scales draining of colour as a panicked lump rose in his throat. "You're endangering the movement!"

The crows stared at him for a moment, then one said, "Nice tail," and the rest cawed in delight.

"*Get out!*" Gilbert yelled, wondering if he dared try singeing them. But that really went against his non-violent values.

The birds looked at each other, then the largest one said, "Nah," and they turned their attention back to the biscuits, cawing around mouthfuls of sugary almond goodness and shouting something about baps.

"Cease and desist!" Gilbert shouted. "Stand down! Um ... Look, just *stop*, okay?"

They didn't even look up, and Bertie shook his head, covering his beak with one claw.

"This is painful," he said, and just as Gilbert decided he was going to have to free Bertie and make a run for it, leaving the crows to their rampage, Carlotta walked into the kitchen.

"Uh-oh," Bertie said.

"What the *hell* is going on?" she screamed, dropping her bag on the floor. The crows launched themselves off the biscuits, scattering crumbs and icing sugar and feathers everywhere. "*Philip!* Did you leave the bloody door open? I swear to God—"

"Nice buns!" one of the crows screeched.

"Work it, baby!" another yelled, swooping low over Carlotta's head.

"You!" she roared, and Gilbert cowered on the floor, but she was pointing at Bertie. "You taught them this!"

"Me?" Bertie said, leaning back on his perch.

Gilbert considered the situation, then dived out the door under the cover of the crows, who, crazed on sugar and the delights of home invasion, were swooping around the big open plan room, gleefully screaming expressions he was pretty sure he shouldn't learn.

"Hey!" Bertie yelled after him. "Get your scaly—" he stopped, looking at Carlotta. "Bertie want a biscuit," he said weakly.

"You'll get a feather duster!" she shouted at him, grabbing a tea towel and giving chase to the crows. "I'll turn you into one myself, you obscene, flea-ridden excuse for a bird!"

"Harsh," Bertie muttered, and glared out the door at Gilbert, who was lingering on the edge of the patio, camouflaged amongst the shrubbery. Gilbert gave a guilty little shrug. One had to expect some setbacks. Not every mission could go smoothly. He just wished it hadn't been Carlotta's house it had gone so very un-smoothly in. She always gave him extra mince pies before Mortimer could eat them all.

However, one had to consider the integrity of the overall movement, not just the individual mission. He slipped away into the fading afternoon, keeping to the grey shadows of the walls and looking for more victims of captivity.

He'd make her a special tree topper. That should fix things.

Behind him, a crow shrieked, "Show us your baps, love!" and Carlotta gave a war cry that set the crows screaming and him running a little faster. He might make that a tree topper, some baubles, and maybe some of the new jewellery he'd been working on.

Just in case.

AMARETTI ESPRESSO BISCUITS

Okay, amaretti biscuits are not really my favourite of treats. I find them intensely sweet and overwhelmingly almond-y, and they exist on such a range from shatter-under-your-bite to stick-to-your-teeth that I never know what to expect from them.

However, as I have a friend who adores them, I have made them more than once, and they have been voted excellent every time. Which, considering she's French and lives near enough to the Italian border that she can get the real thing any time, I feel rather flattered by. And, honestly, they look fancy. They sound fancy. They're just *fancy*. I mean, "Would you care for an amaretti with your espresso?" just sounds that much *fancier* than, "Want a bikkie with your cuppa?"

So I can definitely embrace them as an excellent gift-giving biscuit that sounds far more complicated than they actually are.

However, I do extend apologies to any Italian readers, as I'm sure these are not the amaretti you know and love. I'm sorry.

- 200 g / 2 ¼ cups ground almonds
- 200 g / 1 cup sugar

- 2 Tbsp espresso powder (optional)
- good pinch of salt
- 2 egg whites
- ¼ tsp lemon juice or white wine vinegar
- ½ tsp almond extract
- icing sugar for rolling

Preheat oven to 150°C / 300°F. Line a heavy baking tray with parchment paper.

Combine the almonds, sugar, espresso powder (if using) and salt. Set aside.

Beat the eggs and vinegar until soft peaks form, then add the dry ingredients and the almond extract. Mix well – don't worry about folding or anything, just get it all mixed in.

Roll the mix into balls of roughly a heaped tablespoon in size, then roll in icing sugar. Pop them on the baking tray, and, once done, flatten the tops a little with the back of a spoon.

Bake for around 25–35 minutes or until the outside is crisping up. Keep an eye on the bottoms, as they can burn easily.

Makes around 24 fancy biscuits that look wonderful in jars as gifts, although they'll want to be eaten within a few days.

5

FIVE GOLD RINGS

Detective Inspector Adams switched the coffeemaker on, squinting in the warm light of the kitchen and running her tongue over her teeth as she watched it tick into life. Something nudged her legs and she looked down at Dandy, his dreadlocked hair flopped so low over his eyes that she couldn't really tell if he was looking back. He was the size of a terrier, and she had to bend down to scratch him between the ears.

"Why so small?" she asked him. "Does that mean something?"

He just wagged his tail and tossed his head a little, giving her a glimpse of deep red eyes glowing like LEDs. She supposed she should be used to them by now, but … She brushed his hair back down to hide them.

"D'you want something?"

His snout drifted toward the coffee machine, then back to her.

"I'm fairly certain no vet in the world recommends coffee as part of a healthy canine diet."

He cocked his head, and she nodded.

"Of course, I can't exactly take a dog only I can see to the vet."

She considered it. "Are you even a dog? Should I flea you? Can *fleas* see you?"

Dandy whined and retreated to the back door.

"Not so keen on that, then." DI Adams turned her attention back to the coffee machine.

Dandy barked, a commanding sound that was far too loud for his current dimensions.

"What?" Dandy tended to come and go as he pleased, irrespective of the limitations of doors. DI Adams had never actually *seen* him walk through a wall or vanish into thin air, but he did something to get wherever he wanted to be. It made life as a dog owner rather easy, although she still couldn't get him to stop climbing trees after squirrels, who definitely *could* see him.

Dandy looked at the door then back at DI Adams, and gave her a sudden glimpse of some truly alarming teeth.

She raised her eyebrows. "Well. We're not having *that.*"

Dandy promptly flopped to the floor and rolled over, exposing a pale belly.

"Soft," she told him, and put a cup under the coffee machine before wandering over to rub his belly. He wriggled in delight, then jumped up and looked pointedly at the door, and back at her.

"This is all very Timmy stuck in the well," she said. "Why can't you talk? Every bloody other thing around here can talk, it seems."

He just looked at her, and she had the absurd feeling he was disappointed in her.

"You're right. It's annoying, all that talking." She unlocked the door and opened it onto deep pre-dawn dark, shivering in the chill wash of fresh air, and he looked up at her, waiting.

"Oh, we're doing this, are we? What's up? You too scared to go out alone?" He just looked at her, and she frowned. She didn't like the idea of that, and she wished she hadn't said it. The words seemed to hang in the air around her. "Alright."

She kicked her feet into her trainers and stepped out into the dark December morning in her pyjama bottoms and a hoody, hugging her arms around herself. The low walls of the garden were iced with frost, and the short grass in the tiny backyard was fragile and pale. Her breath hung before her like the ghosts of unsaid things, and the sky was dark and distant. There were no streetlights on this side of the row of terraced houses, only fields running into the darkness, hemmed by houses and the rough path that ran behind them. Here and there lights peeked out from behind curtained bedroom windows, or flooded from the frosted glass of bathrooms, but most of the houses were still dark. It was too early for this.

"Well?" she said to Dandy, and he stepped delicately down the path, looking back at her. "I'm waiting."

He sniffed the air, casting about for something. The cold was sharp and hungry, but DI Adams didn't move, watching Dandy. She still didn't know why he'd adopted her – and it had definitely been that way around – or why she was the only one who was able to see him. Well, the only *human* someone. The dragons and the cat had no problems seeing him, and they weren't exactly fans. But Dandy had proved himself useful, for the most part, other than a small issue regarding the eating of evidence, and she had a niggling feeling that he knew a lot more than he let on. So she waited.

In the dozing silence of the pre-dawn, the nearby streets were empty, and she barely caught the distant sound of traffic on the main road. It was too early for birds or joggers, and the quiet of it all roared softly in her ears. So when Dandy gave a sudden, full-throated bark and bolted, she jumped so badly that she almost slipped on the icy steps.

"*Jesus!* Dandy, what the hell was that for?" But he was already clearing the low wall from her garden into the neighbour's in one smooth leap, and she watched him go. There was absolutely no way she was running around jumping fences at five in the morning or whatever it was.

Dandy's head appeared over the drystone wall, and he gave a warning bark. He was on his hind legs, front paws on the wall, but even so he must have grown to be able to see over.

"Shh," she hissed, and he barked again. "Dandy, *shut up!*" He burst into a volley of sharp barks, the sort that hit the ear drum like a scream, and a light snapped on behind the curtains next door. "Oh, no. Not him." Dandy cocked his head, his mouth open just slightly. "Bollocks. *Bollocks.*" She zipped her hoody to her chin and ran for the wall. "Fine, you mutt. I'm coming."

By the time she was scrambling over the wall, trying to avoid a well-pruned rose bush, Dandy was already over the next wall into another garden. She followed him, glancing up at her neighbour's window in time to see the bedroom curtain twitch back. "Crap," she hissed, and boosted herself over the wall with rather more speed than grace, then sprinted after Dandy. "Invisible dog. Doesn't need feeding. Doesn't need the vet. So easy! Except for the midnight bloody— Alright, alright. I'm coming." She dodged a veggie patch, almost tripped over an abandoned toy truck, and threw herself at the next wall, which someone had handily topped with a tall wooden fence.

"This is fun," she mumbled, and wondered how Dandy had got over. The same way he climbed trees after squirrels, she supposed. She kept going.

Dandy didn't slow, and he didn't look back once he knew DI Adams was following. He hurdled walls, flowed over fences, raced across ice-crusted patios and splashed happily through fishponds, and DI Adams followed. She stumbled on garden gnomes, bounced off a bird bath, skirted flowerbeds and sent her hands numb on walls and fences. Dogs were barking in their wake, and lights were coming on, and she wished she'd brought her police ID with her. She didn't fancy having the cops called on her. She was fairly certain that everyone at the station except Collins still thought of her as That City Cop, and she didn't fancy being elevated to That City Cop Who Runs Around Gardens In The Dark For No Good Reason.

She scrambled over a final wall, snagging the leg of her PJs on some chicken wire someone had put up, presumably to keep in the chickens who were all *buk-bukk*ing in alarm in their hen house, then dropped ungracefully to the ground on the other side, hitching her trousers up. She glared at Dandy, who was waiting under the streetlight at the end of the lane, where it gave onto the field and met the path that ran behind the houses to the left, and into a stand of old trees on the right.

"You're kidding me," she said. "We ran through half a dozen gardens and we could've just used the path?"

Dandy huffed and started running again, heading for the trees. DI Adams bolted after him, thinking she'd have to start sleeping in a sports bra if this was going to be a regular occurrence.

Dandy angled into the darkness of the trees, long legs eating up the ground. He was definitely bigger, and DI Adams hoped that was just for running efficiency and not because they were about to come up against anything that required being a size or two larger. She plunged into the deep shadows, the solitary streetlight lost behind her, and came to a sharp halt, the ground unseen and treacherous underfoot.

"Dandy?" she whispered. The dark ahead of her was intense, the odd glimpse of lights from the sleeping houses doing nothing more than casting the rest into even more of an impenetrable void. Faintly she could hear the racing pad of Dandy's feet fading, then they stopped. She could have been standing on the edge of an abyss, and a wave of dizziness passed over her. She looked back, reassuring herself that the streetlight was still there. A dog was barking somewhere, and someone was shouting at the dog, and someone else was shouting at either the first shouter or the dog or both, but it was all desperately distant. She looked back into the trees, and all was silence and shadows deep enough to touch.

She licked her lips, tried to whistle, then called, "Dandy?"

No response, just a thickening of the dark, if that was possible. She could feel eyes on her, the skin tightening at the back of her neck. She took a breath, touched her hair wrap, and stepped forward carefully, gravel shifting under her foot with the sound of an avalanche.

"DI Adams, North Yorkshire Police," she said. "Identify yourselves."

The only response was an even deeper silence, and she kept walking carefully, feet finding the path more by instinct than sight. Something moved to her left, a whisper on quick soft feet, and she stopped.

"Show yourselves," she ordered the darkness, although someone could have been standing an arm's length in front of her and she'd never have seen them. No one replied, and she started to step forward again. Movement exploded around her, coming from above as well as all sides, wordless and furious.

DI Adams dropped into a crouch, spinning forward and to the side as she did so, turning to look back at the light as she felt the wind of small things running past. Tiny feet thundered on frozen ground, bigger ones pounding after them, and squat shapes darted in silhouette across the path. Something rushed at her from deeper in the trees and she threw herself sideways, smacking her knees painfully and skinning her palms.

She rolled, raising one hand to protect herself, and Dandy leaped over her, racing for the end of the path. He barked, the sound huge and echoing among the trees, and a chorus of panicked screams answered him. Creatures scattered, heedless of her, and small clawed feet sprinted over her legs and arms as she scrambled up. She lunged into the dark, grabbing blindly, and her hands closed on something small and squirming and so stickily *hot* that she almost dropped it again. The thing wailed, kicking out with what felt a lot like heavy-soled boots, which was painful, but at least better than claws might have been.

"Calm down, calm down," she said, aware she wasn't sounding very calm herself. "I'm not going to hurt you."

The thing screamed, so high-pitched that she flinched, then descended into a babble of fury. DI Adams couldn't make out too many words between the pace of the thing's rant and a strong accent she couldn't quite place, but the ones she did would have made even her mum blush.

"Look, I just need— Oh God." Because a roar of feet was bearing down on her, an unseen stampede. It sounded like a fast, ravenous tide coming in, and she took a step back, holding her captive high. "No one's getting hurt here! I'm a police officer! I— Ow!" Something had just bitten her calf. "Stop that!"

Bodies washed around her feet, grumbling in fury, and the creature in her hands was still shouting almost incomprehensible threats. Sharp claws dug through her pyjama bottoms, and small bodies hauled themselves up her legs, while the trees shook with furious movement above her.

"Stop," she ordered them. "I just want to know what you're doing here." She staggered as something hit her on the shoulder, her hoody protecting her from the claws but not the hiss in her ear. She jerked her head away, and a second body hit her other shoulder, then a third, claws latching into her hair.

"Alright, enough! Enough!" She dropped her captive, knocking away the attackers on her back and covering her head with one hand. "I'm going!" She took an uncertain step, suddenly disoriented and unsure how to escape, then spotted the streetlight and started toward it, dragging her legs through a moving, fuming thicket and hoping she didn't stand on any of them. That wouldn't go far toward improving things. Something hit her back, raking its claws down her neck before it let go, and she swore but kept going, holding her pyjama bottoms up with one hand as clutching paws threatened to pull them down.

It was like wading through toothed mud, clinging and persistent, and she could hear the branches shaking above her, loaded with unseen threat. Every now and then one of them would scream, setting her staggering away from the sound, and a ripple of tittering laughter would wash through the rest. But the path was growing brighter, the circle of the streetlight coming forward to meet her, and suddenly her legs were clear, and she broke into a run.

She didn't stop until she was beyond the trees, the yellow illumination of the streetlight surrounding her and stealing the shadows. Then she spun back to the woods, the light reflecting off small sharp eyes on the ground and in the trees, watching her resentfully. She looked around.

"Dandy. Where's Dandy?" No response, and her throat was suddenly tight. *"Where is he?"*

Silence, then a scuffle, and something small and ragged was flung onto the path, just beyond the trees. For one heart-stopping moment she thought it was a *part*, an ear or a paw, then she realised it was her headscarf, shredded beyond rescue. She scowled at it.

"Where's Dandy?" No reply, and she took a step forward, hands on her hips. "Dammit, you little monsters. Give him back or I swear I'll be back here with … with an exterminator."

The eyes shifted, looking at each other. A low ripple of laughter passed through them.

"Oh, you think that's funny?" She looked around, spotted a rather chewed stick and picked it up, waving it threateningly. "Give me back Dandy. *Now.*"

The eyes exchanged glances, and a few of them started to fade back into the trees.

"No you don't," she snapped, and took a step forward. "Don't you *dare* run away on me."

The eyes stopped fading, but there was still no Dandy. She was going to have to go back in after him. This was great. Just *great*. Bloody ridiculous invisible dog. She started forward, her breath harsh in her throat, and a sharp bark interrupted her. She looked around, the stick still raised over her shoulder, and spotted Dandy standing in the field, his tail wagging gently. She lowered the stick.

"Oh, right," she said. "So you got out just fine and left me in there. Nice."

He *whuff*ed gently, then picked something up off the ground and turned to head along the path toward home. Adams looked at the eyes, and they looked back. There was silence for a moment, then she said, "What *are* you?"

There was no answer, just some more chuckling that raised the hair on her arms. She didn't want to go back in there. But she didn't want to just leave them, either, doing God knew what. She could still feel the weight of them hitting her back, the threat of claws on her neck. They were *dangerous.* Yet she knew dog walkers and runners used the woods all the time, and she was pretty sure she'd have heard if they were being assaulted by mobs of unseen beings. Maybe it was just the company she was keeping.

"Ugh," she said. "Look, just … behave yourselves, okay? Don't make me come back and find you." She gave the stick a final threatening shake and turned to follow Dandy. More laughter followed her, and she sighed. She evidently needed to upgrade her threats.

SHE LET them in the back gate, her legs smarting from the scratches and her knee already starting to stiffen up from the fall. Dandy was back to his more familiar Labrador size, a walking mat of hair that sniffed every fencepost they passed. DI Adams frowned at the back door, which was shut, then tried the handle. It didn't turn.

"No," she said, and jiggled it a bit, as if that'd change anything. "*No*. I'm sure I didn't leave the latch on." She looked at Dandy. "Nip in and get the key, can't you? Go on, make yourself useful." He sat down, watching her expectantly. "You're a rubbish magical dog," she told him.

"Miss?" someone said from over the wall, and she jumped, banging her knee on the door.

"Ow."

"Sorry, I didn't mean to startle you," her neighbour said, staring at her. She had the feeling that even though he knew she was police, he very much wanted to call someone more police-ier than her.

She tried to give him a friendly look rather than a glare, but she wasn't feeling it. "You're fine. What is it?"

"I saw your door open. There was a commotion, you know."

"I know," she said. "I was trying to find out what caused it."

He looked at her PJs and said rather doubtfully, "On your own? That doesn't seem very safe."

"I'm a police officer," she said, trying to smooth her hair and fishing a twig out of it. "It's sort of in the job description."

"I suppose," he said, in a way that suggested he didn't suppose that at all, but wasn't going to argue with some strange woman who'd been running around in the dark in her pyjamas. "Anyway, I saw your door was open, so I dropped the latch for you. Can't be too careful, you know."

DI Adams took a deep breath. "Did you happen to pick up the keys when you did that?"

"Oh." His face, already red in the cold, darkened a shade or two. "No. I assumed you had them on you."

DI Adams nodded, looking at the sky. It was still velvet dark.

"Would you like a cuppa?" her neighbour offered in a small voice.

"No," she said. "But I will use your phone."

SHE WAS SITTING on the front step, Dandy leaning on her, when DI Colin Collins ambled down the street in a big puffy jacket that made his broad frame even larger, carrying a paper bag and with a woolly hat pulled down over his ears.

"Morning," he said.

"Morning," DI Adams said, getting up stiffly.

"Rough night?" he asked, handing her the spare key.

"Rough morning."

"You should leave a key with your neighbour," he said, following her into the house.

"I don't like my neighbours," she said, going straight into the kitchen. The heating had come on, and the little house was warm and welcoming.

"Aw. Knew you liked me," Collins said, putting the bag on the table and taking his jacket off.

"Don't be ridiculous," she said, tipping out the cold coffee and refilling the machine. "Want one?"

"Don't you want to get that sorted first?" he asked, pointing at her face. "That's a right good scratch," he added, when she scowled at him.

"I need coffee." Dandy *whuff*ed at her, and she pointed at him. "And you can bloody well wait. This is all your fault."

"You blame a lot on your invisible dog," Collins said, poking into a cupboard. "Have you got any peroxide or Dettol or something?"

"Well, it *is* his fault. It was just … I'm not even sure what happened, to be honest. What were you doing?" she asked Dandy.

"Where did you *go?*"

Dandy whined, then spat something on the floor.

"Oh, that's weird," Collins said. "That just came out of nowhere."

"It came out of his mouth," DI Adams said, and Collins drew back before he touched it. Dandy spat something else out, then another, then two more, all landing in a little clattering pile except for the last, which rolled across the floor toward the sink. Collins stopped it with his boot and picked it up gingerly, holding it toward the light.

There was a pause, then he said, "Has your invisible dog been robbing jewellery shops?"

"I wouldn't put it past him," DI Adams said, and took her mug from the coffee maker, starting it again for Collins.

"Have you?" Collins asked, addressing the general area of the four remaining gold rings, all a little slobbery and with some bits of grass stuck to them. Dandy thumped his tail.

DI Adams took a grateful sip of coffee and said, "So, Dandy, you were off stealing five gold rings while I fended off … whatever those things were."

Dandy put his head on the side.

"They ruined my favourite headscarf," she told him. "Never mind my PJs."

Dandy whined.

"I threatened them for you! And you were *thieving.*"

Dandy hung his head, but she was fairly sure his eyes were on her coffee.

"Sounds like you were a decoy," Collins said. "Bloody clever, your invisible dog." He opened the paper bag and took out two muffins, releasing a whiff of brown sugar and ginger into the kitchen. "Breakfast?"

DI Adams sat down opposite him, still scowling at Dandy. *"Bad dog,"* she said.

"Eat your muffin," Collins said, and went to fetch the other coffee cup.

DI Adams turned her scowl on him, but broke the muffin in two anyway. It was still faintly warm, scattered with nuts and fruit, and tasted of Christmas.

Collins rinsed the rings in the sink and set them in the middle of the table, glittering in the mellow light. "So," he said. "What do we do with these?"

DI Adams looked at Dandy. "Well?" she said, but he just looked hopefully at the coffee machine. She turned back to Collins. "I bet it's something to do with the Toot Hansell."

"How could five gold rings found in a wood in Skipton have *anything* to do with Toot Hansell?" he asked, breaking his own muffin open.

"The whole thing was weird," she said. "And there were critters. Plus, invisible dog. It's totally Toot Hansell. And probably the Women's bloody Institute, too."

He popped some muffin in his mouth and nodded. "Can't have one without the other. Do you have any butter? This'd go well with a bit of butter."

She waved at the fridge and took another sip of coffee. Of course it was Toot Hansell. It was *always* Toot Hansell.

On the floor, Dandy sighed and looked at the coffeemaker, then gave up and lay down with his head on DI Adams' bare foot, sighing to himself. Humans never took a hint.

CHRISTMAS BREAKFAST MUFFINS

Many years ago, I used to cook on charter yachts in the Caribbean. I can only assume I was much more organised back then, and better at both shopping lists and timing, as the thought of trying to shop for a week's worth of meals for ten guests, let alone actually follow recipes and remember what meal goes where, *and* get everything on the table at roughly the right time, three times a day, is terrifying now.

However, what is not terrifying is the idea of muffins.

Hang on. There's a connection here, I promise.

I used to make breakfast breads or muffins every day, to go with whatever cooked breakfast was on offer. And while I tried many different variations of breads over my time, the one thing that never changed (once I happened on the recipe), was the muffins.

They are simple, adaptable, and excellent. You can throw any sort of chopped fruit at them and they'll take it. You can blend peanut butter with the butter, and they'll accept it. You can turn them into mocha muffins, or stuff them with jam, or cram them with spices. All good.

Every single time, they rise prettily, bake perfectly, and have a nice delicate crumb that makes it entirely possible to eat multiple muffins in one sitting. Not me, obviously. That would be the guests. Ahem.

And so when it came to a Christmas variation, I wasn't exactly going to look for a different recipe, was I?

No, I was not.

Here we are, then. Easy, reliable muffins for the win.

For the crumble topping:

- 50 g / ⅓ cup flour
- 25 g / 2 packed Tbsp dark brown sugar
- 35 g / 2 ½ Tbsp / 1 ¼ oz butter
- 50 g / ½ cup walnuts, chopped
- some ginger and cinnamon to taste

Combine the flour, sugar, and spices, then rub the butter in until the mix resembles crumbs and, if squished together, holds its shape a little. Mix in the walnuts and set aside.

For the muffins:

- 190 g / 1 ½ cups flour
- 1 ½ tsp baking powder
- ¼ tsp baking soda
- ¼ tsp salt
- 1 tsp cinnamon
- ½ tsp ground ginger
- pinch ground cloves
- good grating of nutmeg – about ½ tsp
- 70 g / 5 Tbsp / 2 ½ oz butter
- 90 g / ½ cup dark brown sugar

- 1 Tbsp treacle
- 1 egg
- 200 mL / ¾ cup yoghurt
- 100 g / a bit under ½ cup chopped dates

Preheat oven to 180°C / 350°F. Prepare a muffin tin by oiling and flouring, or lining.

Sift or whisk together dry ingredients. Set aside.

Beat butter, sugar and treacle for as long as you have patience for – honestly, I've never got it to the point of creaminess, and it's still always worked. Just show willing. It'll be fine.

Add the egg and beat briefly – it won't look combined. Don't worry about it.

With the mixer on low, or using a wooden spoon, mix in half the yoghurt till mostly combined, followed by half the dry ingredients. Repeat, and mix gently until just combined. Add the dates and fold in – it'll be a thick batter.

Dollop into your prepared tin – this gives 10 tidy little muffins, or 6 huge ones. It doubles easily, too. Whichever way you go, don't fuss about smoothing the mix down. Just chuck a generous amount of crumble over the top. As the muffins rise it'll slide down and get embedded in the sides, which is glorious.

Bake for 25–35 minutes, depending on the size – I usually check with a skewer after 20 minutes. Best eaten warm, but you can reheat them the next day. Plus they freeze easily. See? Friendly little muffins.

6

SIX GEESE A-LAYING

Miriam grated crumbling cheddar cheese onto the breadboard, wondering vaguely at what point a grater became too rusty to use. She did clean any loose rust off before grating anything, so it wasn't as if there was rust going *into* the food. Well, not much, anyway. She eyed her pile of cheese critically, grated a little more, then knocked the old box grater clean before popping it in the sink and going to check the onions sautéing softly on the cooker.

"Almost," she murmured, and popped some bread in the toaster before starting the roux. She knew that *technically* there shouldn't be onions and garlic in the roux, but *technically* was both a boring way to cook and not a method she'd ever embraced, so onions and garlic it was.

She threw in some beer and cream, more by eye than with any sort of measurement, then added the cheese and stirred, humming to herself and adding a little extra wiggle when "Fairytale of New York" came on the radio. Anything other than "All I Want For Christmas". Honestly, you'd think it was the only Christmas song ever released, some days.

The song finished as the toast popped up, and Miriam turned to grab it, then hesitated. She could do with some thyme. Thyme always made things that tiny bit tastier. She looked at the kitchen windows, the dark panes reflecting her own slightly pink face back at her. Her hair had come undone from her scarf on one side and was bushing out in messy curls. She tucked it back in place absently. The thyme was in a pot just outside the back door. She wouldn't even need a coat.

Still she hesitated. This was the problem with being Sensitive. She might not be able to tell the future or talk to spirits (and her tarot business was based much more on reading people than reading cards), but she most certainly felt things that others didn't. And what she'd been feeling for a while was that something was Not Quite Right, which made the idea of venturing out into the dark for the sake of some thyme rather daunting.

She looked at the pot, then picked up the half-empty beer bottle and took a healthy swig. It was *her* garden. She wasn't going to be scared out of going into her own garden by some half-formed feeling that things were *off*. Whatever was out there – and there probably wasn't anything out there – was going to just have to behave themselves, or they'd get it with the kitchen scissors.

Miriam nodded to herself firmly, picked up said scissors, kicked into her flip-flops and opened the kitchen door into the whispering, textured night.

There was a low, cold wind, and it rattled the bare branches of the apple trees and rasped the hard leaves of the bay bushes together like bones. The brook beyond the gate chuckled in the low, unpleasant tones of an angry gossip, and somewhere twigs were clattering against a window petulantly. Miriam stood on the doorstep, her shadow stretching long and hulking across the cold ground, waiting. She could see the thyme huddled in its pot to the left of the door, just a few paces away, but she didn't move. Not yet.

The sense of things not being right had started the other week, when Alice and Jasmine had had that strange encounter with turtles, of all things, in the village square, and it had only grown with the rude French lizards. The magical Folk of the world are *faint*, and keep to themselves. Generally speaking, only those who expect to see them, do. Most humans don't expect to see dragons or dryads or anything other than regular, human-y things, so they don't notice a whole world of creatures existing alongside them. This faintness was how the Folk had stayed undiscovered (and, in Miriam's mind, un-dissected by shadowy government agencies) for centuries. Toot Hansell, of course, with its river-girt village and bottomless duck pond and dragons was a little *different*, but even so, only the Women's Institute knew to expect Folk. Which made this sudden rash of strangeness worrying, to say the least.

Miriam shivered, and hugged her oversized cardigan a little tighter around her, then stepped slowly out into the dark. Everything was off balance, like the ground might suddenly shift underneath her. She glanced around. She'd never really felt threatened by Folk – other than the goblins, of course. But that had been more of a business issue.

The shadows were deep around the old table and chairs in the middle of the flowerbeds, and the wooden arch the roses grew over in the summer had taken on a rather unhappy lean after the last storm. Still nothing jumped out at her, so she took a deep breath and strode to the thyme pot, crouching down to snip a few sprigs with cold fingers, the back of her neck itching and exposed.

It was a matter of moments to get what she needed, and she straightened up, turning back to the kitchen with a little gasp of relief. And she was almost at the door when she heard it. A small but very clear splash, followed by a grumble. It was the sort of grumble someone makes when they're having a very bad day indeed, and their patience is all but gone. Miriam stared at the warm, inviting rug on the kitchen floor and considered ignoring the grumble. She had rarebit ready to go inside, and the remains of the beer, and it was cold and dark out here. Plus, no one said she *had* to help someone who was out in her garden, grumbling.

There was a long-suffering sigh, and some smaller, more irritated splashing, and Miriam felt a little irritated herself. Someone was sitting in her fishpond, sighing loudly and being grumpy. And she hadn't had any fish in the pond for years, but it did breed a very healthy population of tadpoles every spring. She didn't want to upset what might be quite a delicate ecosystem in there. She heaved a sigh and turned down the path, the kitchen scissors gripped firmly in one hand and the thyme in the other.

THE POND WAS in the centre of what had once been an ornamental lawn and was now the site of Miriam's large herb garden, and she picked her way carefully across the old flagstone path toward it, her way faintly lit by the light leaking from the kitchen. She couldn't see anything in the pond just yet, which at least ruled out the possibility of a repeat of the abominable snow creatures. As did the lack of snow, she supposed, but in Toot Hansell these days she'd found it was best not to rule anything out.

She stopped at the edge of the pond, frowning at it. It wasn't big – in fact, "pond" was probably a slightly grand name for it – but it was generously fringed with lilies and deep enough that Rose's Great Dane could only just stand in it. Which he did, almost every time he came over, snapping at frogs and stray leaves with equal enthusiasm.

"Hello?" Miriam said, but her voice came out a little uneven, so she swallowed and said it again, trying to express in those two syllables that it was cold out, she was displeased with strangers using her fishpond without permission, and that she was essentially a friendly person who would prefer not to argue about anything, but she *was* armed, so there better not be any funny business.

There was no response for a moment, then a thin, pale hand floated slowly to the surface of the dark water. Miriam squeaked and clutched the front of her cardigan with both hands, crushing the thyme and almost stabbing herself with the scissors. There was a *body* in her fishpond! Who *ever* had put a body in her fishpond?

"Oh *no*," she whispered. There'd be an investigation. There'd be an investigation, and she'd absolutely go to jail this time, because it was *her* fishpond, and she didn't have any sort of alibi, and she still wasn't sure the detective inspector had quite forgiven her for the poisonous herbs in her garden, and—

The hand waved languidly in her direction, interrupting her train of thought. She gasped. There was a *living dead* person in her fishpond! Why did she have a living dead person in her pond? How did one explain that to the neighbours? And what did one feed a living dead person? She had some lamb in the freezer, but if they wanted anything fresher, then the butcher's was already closed.

The hand was joined by the top of a slightly slimy head, which rose to reveal large, pale, and rather protuberant eyes.

"Oh," Miriam said, sagging a little and easing her grip on the scissors. "It's you."

"It's me," the sprite said, lifting herself up so her mouth was clear of the water, her teeth small and sharp in the low light. "Where are the fish?"

"You scared me," Miriam said, folding her arms across her chest. "I thought you were a dead person!"

"Why would there be a dead person in your pond?" the sprite asked. "Unless they starved from lack of fish, of course."

Miriam frowned at her. "You can't just go sneaking around in other people's ponds. And I don't have fish anymore— Wait. Did you eat all my fish? Is that where they went?"

"No," the sprite said, fiddling with a water lily and not looking at Miriam. Her hands were webbed and faintly green, but Miriam still felt that thinking they belonged to a dead person was a mistake anyone could have made.

"It's Nellie, isn't it?" Miriam said, and the sprite nodded vaguely. "What are you doing here?"

"There's no tiddy 'uns here," Nellie said. "Everywhere else seems to have them, and they're *so* boring." She put on a high, squeaking voice. "Ooh, you're making things slimy. Ooh, you're stirring up the mud. Ooh, don't eat our … reeds." She shot Miriam a quick look from unblinking eyes.

Miriam nodded. "I can see that must be exhausting. But you usually live in the duck pond on the green. Why aren't you there?"

"*Geese,*" Nellie said meaningfully.

Miriam nodded, then frowned. "But there's always geese. Some of them live there."

"Six," Nellie confirmed.

"I don't understand, then. Why are they a problem now?" Although, in her mind, geese were always at least a *bit* of a problem. It seemed to be in their nature.

"They're laying."

Miriam blinked. "*Now?* In December?"

The sprite raised both hands and let them splash back down again. "I know! And they're being *so* unreasonable. I mean, we usually have an arrangement, you know? We each keep to ourselves, and we all keep tiddy 'uns or any other interlopers out of the pond."

Miriam thought the ducks were rather lucky they got to use the pond at all, then. And the model boat enthusiasts.

"But now they mob me every time I surface," Nellie continued. "Look!" She turned her head and pointed to a patch of hair that looked just as lank and slimy as the rest. "Look at that!"

"Oh dear," Miriam said. "I see." And she supposed she might, if the light were better. Either way, the sprite was very upset about it.

"Something's up," Nellie said. "Something's *off*. It's in the water."

Miriam blinked. "Something *is* off."

Nellie stared at her. "What – you feel it too?"

"A little." They looked at each other for a moment longer, and Miriam wanted to ask how the sprite felt it. Was it the same way she did, colours changing and noises taking on different meaning, as if the world were writing her notes she couldn't quite interpret? Or was it clearer for the sprite? And how did the sprite stay out in the world on the bad days, when everything felt raw and rough-edged, and all one wanted to do was curl up at home with a book and maybe some cheesy puffs?

But that seemed … complicated, so instead she just said, "You can stay in the pond, if you want."

"Thanks," Nellie said, and looked around. "Maybe I can get a sparrow in the morning, or something."

Miriam made a small gagging sound. "Do you like rarebit?" she asked.

"Rabbit? Ooh, lovely. They don't usually come close enough to the pond," Nellie said, and flexed her fingers.

"Ew. No. *Rare*bit."

Nellie frowned. "Is that like halibut? I had that once, when I visited my cousin in Blackpool."

"No, it's not really like halibut. Well, not at all like it, actually. It's cheese, mostly."

"Cheese?"

"Yes. Cheese is made from—"

"I know what it *is*," the sprite said, tossing her hair rather undramatically. "Everyone eats cheese sandwiches by the pond."

"Well, do you *like* it?" Miriam demanded.

"I don't know. Probably not. It's not fish, is it?"

Miriam swallowed the voice of her mother, which wanted her

to say, *You'll get what you're given and be happy about it,* and instead said, "It's always good to broaden one's horizons. I'll be back in a moment."

And she turned and hurried back to the house before she could lose her resolve and tell the sprite she had some smoked salmon in the fridge, set aside for her Sunday lunch.

A FAT CANDLE nestling in an old jam jar cast a pale circle of light on the flagstone beneath it, creating an oasis in the darkness. The kitchen windows glowed warm and welcoming at the end of the path, and Miriam tucked her old sleeping bag more firmly around her, then resettled her plate of rarebit on her knees.

The sprite sat at the side of the fishpond, one faintly scaled leg dangling in the water and the other tucked underneath her, eyeing her toast suspiciously.

"It'll go cold," Miriam said, taking a sip of beer. She'd shared it out in two cups, and it hadn't gone far. She supposed that was a good thing, though. Who knew if sprites could handle their drink?

"This is unacceptable," Nellie said.

"*Excuse* me? You haven't even tried it!"

"Not the raw-nit."

"Rarebit."

"Whatever. No, I mean, this whole laying geese thing. I've been chased out of my own home!"

Miriam nodded. "That is rather unfair." She took a bite of her own rarebit. It was just as it should be, rich and tangy and comforting, with the hint of thyme lingering on the edges. She gave a satisfied sigh and snuggled more firmly into the sleeping bag.

"Unfair doesn't even begin to cover it," Nellie said. "And I tell you, if there's disruption in the water, there's disruption *every-where*. It'll spread, you know. The waters connect everything."

"What do you think is causing it?" Miriam asked.

Nellie shrugged. "I don't know. But everything's … too alive. Too worked up. The gnomes are fighting with the pixies and the imps are trying to take them all on. The dryads are getting their moss in a knot and I swear I heard a skriker howl the other night."

"Is that bad?" Miriam asked around a mouthful of rarebit.

"It's not good. It's like all the magic in the area is fizzing to the surface, and I don't know why. We're going to have abominable snow creatures again at this rate."

"Oh *dear*."

"Yeah." Nellie finally took a bite of rarebit and swallowed it whole, then gagged. "It's dry."

"You're meant to chew it."

Nellie stared at her. "I don't chew fish."

"You have to chew this."

"Fine." Nellie took another bite and chewed in an exaggerated way, giving Miriam a few more glimpses of those teeth that she really could have done without. She shook her head and went back to her own dinner, the cold nipping her cheeks but her woolly hat keeping her ears warm. They were both silent for a while, and Nellie didn't say anything else until she'd eaten the last of the rarebit and licked the plate clean. Then she put it down and said, "I can't stay here forever. We need to sort this out."

"We?" Miriam said.

"Yeah. You're in with the dragons. See if they can do something. Just keep that damn cat out of it all."

"Thompson? He's not so bad."

"He steals my fish."

"Oh." Miriam nodded. "I can ask the dragons, then. I'm sure they'll know what to do about it all."

The sprite shrugged. "They've got to be good for something,

right?" She slid into the pond and submerged, leaving Miriam staring at the still, dark surface, tiny ripples distorting the reflection of the candle. She sighed, finished the last of her beer, and got up, untangling herself from the sleeping bag, then collected the plates to head back to the house. She was just starting up the path when there was a soft splash in the pond and Nellie said, "Hey."

"Yes?" Miriam asked, bracing herself for more complaints about the lack of fish and deciding she really did need to get this geese thing sorted as soon as possible.

"Thanks," the sprite said, and scratched her cheek. "For letting me stay. I mean, all the waters of the village are technically mine, but, you know. Thanks anyway."

"Of course," Miriam said. "Any time."

"And for the roar-git thing. It was good. For not being fish."

"You're welcome," Miriam said, and the sprite nodded, then vanished again, leaving Miriam alone in the dark, whispering garden, feeling magic curling and tugging in the night like a tide.

Yes, the dragons would have to be consulted. But she had a rather more direct idea for dealing with the geese, and she was going to take it.

Because if Nellie stayed here too much longer Miriam would just end up giving her the smoked salmon, and she was rather looking forward to it. There had to be a limit to one's hospitality, after all.

Humming to herself softly, Miriam went into the warm cocoon of the kitchen and shut the night out, although it seemed a little less unfriendly now, that sense of not-rightness a little less overwhelming. She would have a tea, she decided, and a piece of fruit cake.

She wondered what a sprite's opinion on fruit cake might be. She imagined not high.

WELSH RAREBIT

So I will admit to briefly considering renaming this "Yorkshire rarebit", but then I remembered that Welsh people have dragons too, and at least one Welsh person knows where I live (hi, Sam!), so I thought better of it. Besides, it sounds wrong.

Welsh rarebit has been around an exceptionally long time, with records of it popping up in the first half of the eighteenth century, when it was referred to as Welsh rabbit, apparently due to the Welsh being so poor that it was their substitute for the animal.

To eat, I mean. They weren't sticking cheesy toast all over the fields because they didn't have any actual rabbits.

However it may have started out, rarebit is no poor substitute for *anything*. It's delightfully rich, with a tanginess that stops the cheese being too cloying, and has so many variations that you can find one to suit just about any preference.

As long as your preferences include cheese, of course. It's not a dish for the lactose intolerant, vegans, or general cheese-haters.

For me personally, chucking some lightly wilted spinach and sautéed mushrooms under the sauce make for an absolutely perfect comfort meal. You may prefer to garnish with an egg, or to add bacon, or ham, or sliced tomatoes, or pretty much anything else that takes your fancy.

And speaking of cheese, I would imagine that it would traditionally be made with a Welsh cheese like Caerphilly. I use extra-mature cheddar, because it's lovely, and you can use whatever takes your fancy. Similarly with the liquid – I use milk, but beer is more common. I would say that when using the milk you do need to add a little more sharpness, which is where I like throwing in some hot sauce. I've also seen recipes call for cream, but I think that'd be *very* rich.

- 30 g / 2 Tbsp / 1 oz butter
- 30 g / 3 Tbsp flour
- 1 tsp mustard (seeded, Dijon or English, to taste)
- 60 mL / ¼ cup beer / ale / milk
- Worcestershire sauce, to taste
- Hot sauce, to taste
- 180 g / 1 ⅓ cups / 6 ¼ oz grated cheese
- 2 egg yolks, beaten
- 4 slices of bread

Toast your bread and set aside on a grill pan. Get your grill heated up and ready to go.

Melt the butter in a saucepan, then add the flour, stirring vigorously to form a paste. Mix in your mustard, then add your beer or milk gradually, stirring well after each addition to make sure it's combined before adding more.

Once all the liquid is in, add the Worcestershire and hot sauce, then allow to thicken before adding the grated cheese. Stir constantly while the cheese melts down to form a smooth sauce. Lovely!

Remove from the heat and beat in the egg yolks, then give the mix a few minutes to cool and thicken before spooning it onto your toast (it should spread nicely rather than running everywhere. Give it a little longer to sit if need be).

Pop under the grill until the cheese mix is bubbling and browned.

Serves two generously, but you can also use just half the mix and pop the rest in the fridge in case of rarebit emergencies. You never know.

7

SEVEN SWANS A-SWIMMING

"No," DI Adams said, staring at the duck pond with her arms crossed over her chest. It was raining, a hard unpleasant rain that was close to sleet, and it pinged off her bright yellow police jacket aggressively.

"You can't just say *no*," Collins said. "We've not even discussed a plan yet." His face was pink in the cold, and rain dripped off his nose.

"I can. I just did. We're *detectives*, not ... whoever should be doing this."

He rocked on his heels, peering at the pond from the patchy shelter of his hood. They were both standing at a respectful distance, and the rest of the green was empty, as all sensible people would be home with a cup of something hot, rather than out here in this. Yet here they were.

"Sometimes, Adams, you just have to muck in. We're not—"

"A big city cop shop, I know." She sighed. "But can't it wait until the council gets here? Or can't we call the RSPB or someone?"

"Bird protection?" He frowned. "They're not endangered, though, are they?"

"No, they're just endangering every bloody other person," DI Adams said, looking at the road beyond the small, rocky slope above the duck pond. She couldn't see it from this angle, but someone had dropped a shopping bag on the pavement and fled. She and Collins had marked a wide perimeter around the oranges and little packets of nuts spilling from the bag, blocking the pavement and part of the road with orange cones. The abandoned groceries looked a little forlorn, like they should be part of a murder scene, not a … whatever this was. She wondered if she might prefer a murder scene, now she thought about it.

"Look, Aunty Miriam called me. She said it was urgent." Collins scratched his chin. "Also something about smoked salmon, but I didn't get that bit."

"And you told the council, because duck ponds are their deal, so why are we here again?"

"Because they can't get here till this afternoon, and we can't just *leave* it."

DI Adams scowled at him. "You couldn't have sent a couple of constables?"

He shrugged. "Do we want a couple of constables poking around Toot Hansell, wondering why geese are laying in December and why the duck pond suddenly has swans?"

DI Adams growled, and Dandy jumped, looking up at her with a little whine. The rain was staining his grey coat a dark steel colour, which was going to be just great for her car. Being an invisible dog apparently had no effect on his ability to transport muck.

"There we go, then," Collins said, much too happily, as far as DI Adams was concerned. You'd think he *liked* this, traipsing around in his wellies like dealing with stray waterfowl was a highlight of the job. She wondered again what she'd been thinking, transferring from Leeds. Surely that had been far enough from London. She hadn't needed to move to *Skipton* as well. But she fell into step with him as they started toward the pond.

"You know they can break your arm, right? Swans, I mean. And geese are used as guard dogs because they're so bloody vicious."

He snorted. "We're not going to disturb them. We're just going to put a perimeter around the area to keep anyone out, then leave it for the council to sort out. One traumatised poodle and two kids with skinned knees and a life-long phobia of birds is plenty for one morning."

"Like a bit of plastic fencing's going to stop them," DI Adams muttered, but she forced a thigh-high metal stake into the soggy ground before marching a couple of paces to the left to do the next one. Collins veered away to the right with his own bundle of stakes, both of them working methodically and keeping half an eye on the birds as they did so.

Miriam had called Collins that morning to tell him that she had a disgruntled sprite in her fishpond who refused to even go and look at the duckpond, as she claimed the rarebit had given her indigestion. Miriam and Alice had gone to see if the geese had calmed down, and had instead found a raging battle in progress between the aforementioned birds and seven swans, who had appeared from nowhere and were apparently in no mood to return there. The only time they seemed to stop fighting was when anyone came even remotely close to the pond, at which point the birds joined forces to become one terrifying avian battalion.

They seemed to have come to some sort of truce by the time the inspectors had arrived, though. DI Adams could see white and grey feathers littering the pond like fluffy confetti, but the birds had withdrawn to opposing sides of the water, occasionally hissing at each other just to keep the tension up. Four of the geese were sitting in the reeds, presumably on nests, leaving only two to fend off the interlopers. The fact that they didn't seem to be having any problems doing so just confirmed to her exactly how formidable the geese were, and she looked around uneasily, making sure she had a good line of retreat.

Dandy nudged her leg, and she scowled down at him. Her knee was still a bit achy, and she hadn't slept well the night before. She'd kept checking out the window in case there were eyes in the trees. "What? You're not forgiven, you know. You're a thief, and I'm out here chasing overgrown chickens. I don't like it."

"You don't say," Collins said beside her, and she jumped. "Cable ties." He handed her a bundle and ambled back to the roll of orange plastic fencing they'd left on the ground where they started.

DI Adams grumbled, but kept going, spacing the stakes evenly, her hands stinging under the assault of the rain, and a nasty trickle of cold water sneaking down her collar where her hood kept blowing back. She followed the curve of the pond at a safe distance, across the neat grass of the green and into the trees and pleasant undergrowth that framed it on either side. It was tougher going once she was under cover, the terrain all rocks and roots, and after stabbing the ground in a variety of places she gave up and went back for the fencing roll. Collins was already starting to cable-tie it to the stakes on his side.

"The ground's too hard in there," she told him. "We'll have to use the trees instead."

"Same on this side," Collins said. "That'll be good enough. Silly beggars if they go clambering through there anyway."

"It's the General Public we're talking about," she pointed out.

"Which means we'll be lucky if no one climbs the fence before we're done," he said, and grinned.

She snorted, and got to work unrolling the fencing on her side and cable-tying it to the stakes. It didn't have to be perfect. It just had to be enough to keep everyone clear until the bloody council turned up and did whatever they did to move on six broody geese and seven irate swans.

Rather them than her.

SHE WAS IN THE TREES, pretending to ignore the large dollops of rain the branches kept flinging at her, and hissing at Dandy to stop digging up what looked like some sort of exotic and probably endangered fern, all while threading fencing through the undergrowth and trying to find suitable-sized trees to attach it to, when someone shouted, "What's going on here, then?"

She looked up, peering from the shelter of her hood at a man standing on the pavement just beyond the low iron railings that separated the road and the rocky slope above the pond. *Inside* their perimeter of cones, because of course he was.

"Is this yours?" he called, pointing at the spilled bag. "Should I get it for you? Or is it, like, evidence?"

"Oh, bollocks," she said. The birds were muttering, long necks rising like sea serpents from the pond and reeds. "Move back!" she shouted. "Back behind the cones, sir!"

"Back!" Collins shouted, as the man craned to look at them. "We need you behind the cones *now!*"

"But should I grab this?" the man asked, pointing at the bag. "Only the bread's getting soggy."

The geese were leaving their nests, the swans paddling across the pond, all of them muttering and craning to see their target.

"Move!" DI Adams shouted, dropping the fencing and breaking into a run, stumbling on rocks and hopping through low shrubs. "Move back *now!*"

"Sorry?" he asked, and the swans charged the bank. The geese exploded into an infuriated chorus of honking and thundered after them.

"Back!" Collins bellowed, crashing through the undergrowth like a fluorescent yellow bear. "Back, move *back!*"

"I was only trying to help," the man said, sounding put out, and the birds washed over the rocky slope in a flood of pounding wings and outstretched necks. The man squawked and staggered back as they crested the rise, and Adams burst from the trees and hurdled the low railing with them. She protected her head with one hand and grabbed for the man's arm with the other. She missed, hitting his chest instead as she charged forward, so she just twisted her fingers into the front of his jacket and tried to carry him with her. He stumbled, tripping over his own feet, and slipped from her grasp while wings battered her head and back. Hard beaks struck her shoulders and her legs, and she staggered, trying not to trip over him.

The birds weren't letting up their attack, and DI Adams caught her balance, grabbing the man's shoulder as Collins burst through the feathery assault and seized him from the other side. They dragged him onto the road, then Collins yelped, going to one knee with his hood blown back and his scalp bleeding.

"Cover your head!" DI Adams yelled at him, still dragging the man backward and wondering where the hell Dandy was when you needed some help – or at least a distraction. Collins scrambled back to his feet and staggered after her with his arms over his head, fending the birds off. They were almost to the other side of the street, where her car was parked with its nose pointing in the wrong direction, but still the birds kept coming, and the man on the ground was kicking in alarm but doing absolutely nothing to help her. Collins grabbed hold of him again, and she let go, scrabbling in her pockets for the keys and beeping the car open.

"In!" she shouted, hauling both passenger side doors open. Collins just about threw the man bodily in the back. She sprinted for the pavement, colliding with the nose of the car and almost falling when a beak hit her shoulder like a punch. She caught herself on the wing mirror, narrowly avoided being knocked over by the driver's door as Collins leaned over to throw it open, and dived in. She nearly shut a swan in with them, but booted it back with a yelp as it lunged for her, then slammed the door just before a goose struck the window. Then all was abruptly quiet inside but for their panicked breathing, and the sharp staccato of beaks and wings on the car outside.

DI Adams wiped her face with a hand that, she was pleased to see, was only shaking slightly, and shouted, "Don't you *dare* break my windscreen, you feral bloody chickens!" The man in the back squawked as if she'd been addressing him, and she looked at Collins. He was wiping blood from his head with a handkerchief, feathers stuck to his short-cropped hair. She blinked. "You have a hanky."

"Far more eco-friendly than a tissue," he said, pressing it in place.

"Do you have spectacles on a string, too?" she asked, and he snorted, then they both jumped as one of the birds hit the windscreen with a crack so sharp DI Adams was surprised it didn't shatter. "Stop that!"

"Try the horn," Collins suggested.

She hit the horn, a long blast, but the birds just honked back and renewed their assault. There was a *snap* from the back window, the sound of gravel being flung at high speed, and a rather threatening chip appeared, a little spiderweb of cracks radiating from it. The man in the back seat screamed and tried to climb into the front with them. Collins pushed him back.

"Please sit down, sir."

The man did, mostly in the footwell.

"We're leaving," DI Adams said. "That'll shift them." She reached for the keys, but they weren't there. She patted her pockets.

"Tell me you didn't drop them," Collins said.

She rubbed her jaw. "To be fair, we *were* being assaulted." She tried the horn again. "Get *off!*"

"New tactic," Collins said, as the birds flew into an even more frenzied attack. "Let's be really, really quiet."

They fell silent, staring at the geese and swans as they struggled for prime position in front of the windscreen or peered angrily in the side windows. DI Adams couldn't shake the feeling that they looked a little smug, and two of them had hold of one of the windscreen wipers, trying to pull it off. She sighed.

"How the hell do I put this through the insurance?"

"Act of God?" Collins suggested.

"Act of Toot Hansell," DI Adams grumbled, and scowled at a swan tapping her side window. "Go away, you horrible monsters."

"I suppose we have to wait for the council," Collins said. "They should be here this afternoon some time."

"Marvellous."

They lapsed back into silence. One of the geese settled itself comfortably on the bonnet and stared unwaveringly at DI Adams. She glared back at it. They waited.

THE BARK CAME WITHOUT WARNING, deep and thundering, and DI Adams almost thought she felt it shake the car like a bass.

"What the hell was *that?*" the man in the back seat demanded, trying to squeeze even lower in the footwell. "What's going *on?*"

"Finally," DI Adams said, as the birds shifted uneasily, turning to look toward the pond.

"Is it him?" Collins asked.

"Yep." She'd never worked out why people sometimes heard Dandy – or dragons – without seeing them, but she thought it was to do with thinking about things too much. Everything one saw was interpreted. Hearing sneaks up on you. And now Dandy stood on the pavement by the pond railings, tall as a Great Dane but twice as wide, his muddy, dreadlocked coat all but brushing the ground under his belly. An egg lay at his feet, and he put one enormous paw on it, waiting.

The new stillness that followed was full of anxious tension, the birds craning their necks toward Dandy and looking at each other. Then one of the geese abandoned the windscreen wiper and leaped off the bonnet, neck out in a tight line of fury as it charged him, hissing wildly. Dandy delicately picked up the egg in his mouth and stepped over the fence, vanishing toward the pond with the goose in pursuit.

The rest of the geese broke a moment later, piling across the road with panicked honks, and the swans lingered a little longer, shuffling around like partygoers who don't want to seem rude but think they might be missing something much better at the party down the block. Finally one waddled across the road, moving with exaggerated casualness. The rest followed in a rush of feathers, and by the time they reached the railing they were all flying. They plunged out of sight, and even through the window DI Adams could hear the fighting restart on the pond. She leaned back in her seat and closed her eyes.

"Bloody hell," Collins said, and opened his door.

"Don't do that!" the man in the back seat yelped. "They might come back!"

DI Adams opened her eyes and twisted in her seat to look at him. "Are you hurt, sir?"

He patted himself down, his eyes wide and his hair sticking in strange directions, and said, "My tailbone hurts. I think I landed on it when you pushed me over. You might have cracked it."

"I doubt it," she said, although she had no idea. "And would you prefer I'd left you there?"

"Well, no," he admitted.

"There we go, then. You're safe to leave, but next time please listen when the police give you instructions." She swung out of the car and opened the back door to wave him out. He emerged rather reluctantly, but then took off in the direction of the pub at a respectable sprint.

Collins fished the car keys out of a drift of feathers and handed them to her. "That was interesting."

"I'm not going back down there," she said. "That's going to have to do."

"We should probably get that shopping bag," he said. "You know, so there's not a repeat performance. And set the cones back up again."

She looked at the cones, rolled into the road and across the pavement. "Go on, then."

"I'm injured." He pointed at his head. "What if I pass out?"

She scowled at him. "I hate geese. I really do."

"Me too."

"Why couldn't it be an invasion of canaries or something?"

"It was the swans that invaded, not the geese."

"Well, I hate them too." She hurried across the road before she could think about it any more, dropping into a crouch as she got closer to the fence in case the damn birds saw her. But they seemed to be otherwise engaged, judging by the clamour from the pond, and she snatched up the bag then hurriedly replaced the cones before running back to safety, one hand out to stop an oncoming car. Not that it was exactly speeding – it inched past them, the driver staring in astonishment at the feather-covered VW Golf and the inspectors, who weren't looking a lot better.

DI Adams dropped the bag in the boot and climbed back into the car. She looked at Collins and his bleeding head. "Do you need a doctor for that?"

"I need a cuppa," he said. "Probably some cake, too. You know, for the shock."

"I don't think we're in short supply of that around here," she said, then yelped as a wet nose stuck itself in her ear. "Dandy! Don't *do* that!"

He whined and sat back, smearing the backseat liberally with mud and feathers.

She sighed, and reached around to scratch his ears. "Good boy. *Good boy.*"

"I know I am," Collins said. "Can we go now?"

"You know I'm not talking to you."

"I can't see anyone else in the car."

Adams shook her head and started the engine, the windscreen wipers grinding into life with the passenger side one lagging unhappily. She wondered if there were any irate geese clauses in her insurance policy.

Miriam's kitchen was so hot that DI Adams thought her clothes might actually be steaming, the big old Aga cooker baking out heat. Dandy lay in front of it with his belly turned to the ceiling, all four paws straight up in the air, and Mortimer sat near the door to the garden with a large mug of tea clutched in both paws. His scales were so grey he blended with the stone floor.

"Mortimer, you can come in a bit further," Beaufort said. "Look at him. He's quite harmless."

"He's not," Mortimer said.

"Well, he's friendly, then," Beaufort said. "To us, at least."

DI Adams picked up another piece of bread. It was still slightly warm and crammed with cranberries and nuts and cheese, and she smeared it with a generous amount of butter before saying, "He is alright, Mortimer. Really."

Dandy opened one red eye and looked at her, then closed it again, and Mortimer shuddered.

"It's that," he said. "The eyes. They make my scales go funny."

"That's a bit off, lad," Beaufort said. "He can't help his eyes."

"They are a bit off-putting," DI Adams said around a mouthful of bread, and Dandy rolled to his belly, looking at her reproachfully. "Sorry. But they are." He huffed and put his chin on his paws.

"I'm sure my head's fine, now, Aunty Miriam," Collins said, trying unsuccessfully to reach the bread. "I think I just need a bite to eat."

"You could have concussion," Miriam said, holding him firmly in place with a packet of frozen peas pressed against his head. "Those horrible birds!"

"They should be sorted now," DI Adams said. "It's all fenced off, and we called the council on the way over. They're bringing some sort of expert and are going to rehome the lot of them."

"Hopefully their expert comes with body armour," Collins said, finally breaking free of Miriam and grabbing a chunk of bread. "But your sprite should be able to go home tonight."

"She's not *my* sprite," Miriam said, putting the peas back in the freezer with rather more energy than was necessary. "She just turned up! *And* she ate my smoked salmon."

"She obviously knew the best person to help her," Collins said, giving his aunt a one-armed hug. "This bread is wonderful, by the way."

"I just can't believe you went and got hurt," Miriam said, sitting down. "It's no good, this."

"But you said there was another problem," Beaufort added, eyeing the bread. DI Adams buttered a slice and handed it to him, and he grinned, showing some very impressive teeth.

"She said there's a magic spill," Miriam said. "But we can go and ask her. She's in the pond still."

Collins looked at the rain streaking the windows, then at DI Adams. "Great," he said, and she sighed.

THEY CLUSTERED around Miriam's fishless pond, the two dragons, the two detectives, and Miriam (Dandy had declined to budge from the Aga), and listened to Nellie explain, her long webbed fingers ticking off the issues of an overflow of magic.

"But how does that happen?" Collins asked, rain dripping off his hood.

She stared at him. "You're the detective."

"This is a little outside my area of expertise," he said, and looked at DI Adams.

She shrugged. "I only have an unreliable invisible dog."

"Fat lot of good you two are," the sprite said, and turned to the dragons. "How about you?"

Mortimer looked at his paws, and Beaufort tapped his talons on the sodden ground. Rain ran off his wings, turning the greens and golds of his scales muted and liquid in the grey light.

"It is Christmas," he said.

"Genius," Nellie said, and he ignored her.

"What does that mean?" DI Adams asked. "Is that some sort of solstice thing?"

"It is Saturnalia," Miriam said. "Yule, even."

Collins gave her a puzzled look, but Beaufort shook his head. "There's a lot of extra belief around at Christmas. People believing in Santa, or kindness, or reconnection, or family. *Really* believing in it, and thinking about it, not like the rest of the year. Believing in every sort of everyday magic."

No one spoke for a moment, then DI Adams said, "That's it? Too much belief? You think *that's* causing all this?"

Beaufort looked at her, an amused gleam in the tarnished gold of his old eyes. "Belief can be extraordinarily powerful, DI Adams. And once it has a certain mass it just keeps going, like a snowball, collecting everything before it."

DI Adams thought of her beak-dented car and the five gold rings locked in her desk at the station while they tried to decide what to do with them, and touched her scratched cheek. "Bollocks," she said. "This is just the start, isn't it?"

"It's not Christmas yet," Beaufort said.

"Bollocks," she said again, with feeling, and Collins heaved a sigh. Then there was nothing but the hiss of rain on leaves and plinking into the pond, and the chatter of the brook beyond the gate.

Eventually Miriam said, "Tea?"

CRANBERRY, WENSLEYDALE & WALNUT NO-KNEAD BREAD

I have a good relationship with baked goods. I like baking them. I like eating them. Win-win, really.

However.

Bread – as in actual, yeasty, magically-rises-due-to-little-yeast-beasts bread – is something I've only come to recently. And, weirdly, I find sourdough much easier, because the recipe I use is so forgiving that I've forgotten it out of the fridge for three times the length it was meant to be out, neglected to fold it when I should, and had complete disasters getting it into the pot (as in only half went in on the first go, and the rest sort of had to be stuck on after), but it still works. It's my sort of bread.

Regular yeast bread, however ... Under-proving. Over-proving. Over-kneading. Under-kneading. Windowpane tests. Strange kneading techniques. And, of course, watching far more *Great British Bake Off* than is good for me, and so knowing that things may look great from the outside, but inside all may be squidgy doom.

Kind of like life, that last one.

But. *But.* There is a glorious recipe that solves all these conundrums. No need to worry about feeding a sourdough starter, or waiting three days for your loaf of bread (even if that is strangely satisfying ... just me? Okay). No kneading terror, or aching arms. Just pure simplicity.

It is ideal for those too intimidated by *Bake Off* to enjoy the art of kneading (me), even if Paul Hollywood would probably shake his head at it. However, I defy anyone to taste this glorious version and say it'd be better with a knead.

And if you want more no-knead bread, this is based off the original Jim Lahey recipe, so if you pop that in your search you will find many, many easy and delightful breads.

- ½ tsp yeast
- 350 mL / 1 ½ cups warm water
- 1 Tbsp honey
- 400 g / 3 ¼ cups bread flour
- 2 tsp salt
- 100 g / ¾ cup dried cranberries
- 100 g / ¾-ish cup / 3 ½ oz Wensleydale cheese, chopped into cubes
- 50 g / ½ cup roughly chopped walnuts
- 1 tsp orange zest to taste
- chopped fresh rosemary (optional)

Combine the yeast, warm water and sugar and leave in a warm place until you have a nice foam going.

Combine the activated yeast mix, flour, and salt. Mix well, then add the fruit, cheese, nuts, zest, and rosemary (if using). Mix well enough to make sure everything's distributed well. It'll be really claggy and rough-looking, but it's meant to be, I promise.

Leave in a covered bowl in a warm place for 18 hours (which means, if you're more organised than me, that you can have it ready to go for breakfast the next day).

After your 18 hours, heat a Dutch oven, casserole dish, or other lidded dish (you can also use a pot with some foil over the top) in the oven at 250°C / 480°F.

Turn your dough onto a floured surface and shape into a rough ball, giving it a smooth-ish top. Transfer the ball onto a sheet of parchment paper and slash the top lightly. Transfer into your heated pot and cover.

Bake for 25 minutes at 250°C / 480°F, then remove the lid and turn down to 225°C / 440°F. Bake a further 10 minutes or so, or until the top's lovely and brown and it sounds hollow when you tap the bottom.

Devour with lashings of butter. It is best if you let it mostly cool first, though, as that means it'll slice without squishing up and getting a doughy texture. This freezes well, so I'd eat it on the day or get it frozen. If you slice it before freezing you can grab a piece and pop it in the toaster any time, and it tastes even better that way, if that's possible.

8

EIGHT MAIDS A-MILKING

Gert padded through the house in her bulldog slippers, pulling her dressing gown tighter as she went. It had been a present from her youngest, and was printed with palm trees and blue seas, which seemed to her an appropriate design for dark winter mornings. The sun wouldn't be up until near enough half-eight, and it'd be gone again by four. Even with all the Christmas lights in the world, a little tropical sunshine in dressing gown form wasn't to be dismissed. It reminded one that warmer days would come. She wondered briefly if she and Murph should take a holiday next year. An overseas one, rather than the usual family ones. Last year they'd gone to her niece's husband's aunt's holiday caravan in Wales, and the year before to her brother's sister-in-law's cousin's cottage in the Highlands. Which had been fun, but it wasn't the Caribbean, was it?

Gert filled the kettle as she wondered what island they might go to, and what direct flights might be like. Murph didn't like the little island-hopper planes. He went a very delicate shade of green as soon as he saw one. She took a mug from the cupboard and the milk from the fridge, going through the ritual of the morning with her mind in other latitudes. Making tea wasn't something she needed to think about.

Or it usually wasn't, until she reached for the tea canister and put her hand on something soft and faintly angular, and definitely alien to her tea-and-biscuits cupboard.

She jerked her hand back, swearing, and blinked at the round-eyed, fixed smile staring back at her. "Bloody elf," she said, and put it on the counter, then pulled the tea out. Murph must be playing around with it again. He'd been quite taken with it when their Darren and his hubby had been up – must be five Christmases ago now. Johan had been doing that ridiculous thing of setting it up for the kids somewhere new every night, and Murph had decided it was so much fun that he'd bought one and made a Facebook account for the damn thing, where he posted photos of more and more complex elf-centric adventures. It had supposedly been to entertain the grandkids, but it hadn't escaped Gert's notice that the elf had acquired a Twitter account before long, too.

He'd stopped the year before last, though. After the whole alpine set-up in the backyard had been destroyed by the neighbour's cats (he'd even bought ice to sculpt lakes, and shaved the stuff to make snow, and the cats had ... well, *defaced* it), he'd sort of lost interest. Done to death, he said. Last year he'd built reindeer shoes instead and gone clumping up and down the streets on Christmas Eve, leaving footprints on lawns until he was chased by the Millers' dogs. No word on what he was planning for this year, but maybe it was back to the elf. She scowled at it. Finding its creepy face staring at her from the tea cupboard was no way to start the morning.

Gert pottered around the kitchen, checking the news on her tablet and drinking her tea, squinting at the calendar on the wall and deciding what to do first. She had the Women's Institute meeting here today. Murph already knew to be out by mid-morning. It was tight enough for ten of them in her low-ceilinged living room, even with the doors pushed open to the dining room. She didn't need him in the way, wedged in the old leather armchair or sprawled on the sofa watching woodworking shows on Netflix.

And she'd be having words about the bloody elf.

BY THE TIME MURPH EMERGED, a slight man in paint-splattered trousers and an old brown jumper with a hole in the elbow and two more on the neck, Gert had the Yorkshire pudding mix already resting in the fridge and was mixing horseradish into cream and chives to go in the puddings with the roast beef. She'd stuff a few with roasted portobellos, too, just to show willing.

"Dinner?" Murph asked hopefully, looking at the side of beef resting in the roasting tin.

"If there's any left over."

He sighed and flicked the kettle on. "With that lot? Not bloody likely."

Gert snorted, and handed him his mug. "I *may* keep some back. And I *may* have made some extra pud mix."

He brightened. "I'll be home early."

"Doesn't mean you'll get your dinner early." She pointed at the elf, now sitting on the windowsill above the sink, wedged between a wilting pot of basil and the washing-up liquid. "Back to the bloody elf, are we?"

Murph stared at it for a moment, then dropped a tea bag in his mug. "No, not this year. I've got something else in mind."

"What was he doing in my cupboard, then?"

"No idea. But he is an elf. Get up to all sorts, they do." He opened the fridge. "Do we have any bacon?"

"Get away with you. The doctor said no more than once a week, remember?"

"*Doctors,*" Murph grumbled, but took a pot of yoghurt instead, ambling about the kitchen with his near-bald head glowing in the overhead lights.

Gert scowled at the elf. There'd be no mischief in *her* kitchen.

GERT TOOK a pile of Christmas napkins and a stack of side plates into the living room, pushed open the sliding doors that closed off the dining room with one hand, and stared at the magazines, newspapers, cardboard boxes of assorted sizes, small bits of wooden dowel, tubes of glue and half-finished tins of paint that were piled on the table. It looked like the nest of a squirrel with crafting aspirations.

"Well, that's helpful," she said to the empty house, and put the plates on the clearest bit of table she could find. One of the newspapers was from June, which showed just how much they'd used the dining room this year. The last meeting she'd hosted had been in the garden. She poked a lidless tube of glue, a stalactite attaching it to the newspaper underneath, and sighed.

She turned to go back to the kitchen and find a crate to throw it all in, then stopped. Something was *off*. The living room didn't look right. Had something happened to the tree? It was still upright, if a little lopsided and a touch threadbare (Gert had got it from her brother-in-law's cousin's nephew, who hadn't exactly said where he was sourcing it, but it had been a bargain), and decorated with two generations' worth of homemade chains and baubles. It was also topped with an octopus, for a reason Gert couldn't quite recall. But that was all as it should be. The bookshelves and mantlepiece were still festooned with lights and tinsel, and the windowsills were still crowded with pinecones that had once been painted gold but were now looking a little tarnished. Nothing was out of place, and yet ...

Gert shook her head, gave the room a look that told it to

behave itself, and started for the kitchen again. Then a flash of colour in the old china display cabinet that had belonged to her gran caught her eye. She sighed.

"Bloody Murph," she said, and opened the cabinet to fish the elf out. He was sitting with the eight china milkmaids she'd inherited from an aunt who'd insisted they were priceless. Gert thought they were priceless in the sense that no one would pay for them, but there they were, with their bonnets and buckets and the elf, who … *"Murph."* It wasn't as if the W.I. were prone to being scandalised, but still. Jasmine would get the giggles and that'd be half the meeting gone before she calmed down. She plucked the elf out and carried him into the kitchen. "I'll think of something for you later."

Like the bin.

THE YORKSHIRE PUDDINGS were set out, ready to be filled at the last moment, the sausage rolls (pre-made, because she wasn't faffing around with that as well as puddings) rested on trays waiting to slide into the oven, and the dining table was laid with cups and plates and condiments, as well as extra mats for the offerings the W.I. would bring with them. Gert wandered from the bathroom into the bedroom, towelling her hair as she went and thinking about what to wear. Her favourite grandchild – not that she *had* favourites, obviously, but if she did, it would be this one – had knitted her a large green jumper with pom-pom baubles stuck all over it. One arm was longer than the other, and the hemline was variable, but it was the thought that counted. She'd wear that.

She was trying to find a dress that didn't clash too badly with the jumper when a clatter from down the hall stopped her. She frowned. Murph shouldn't be back. It was too close to the W.I. showing up. He found any large group unnerving and the W.I. positively terrifying. And the doors were locked. It might not be usual practise for the village, but old habits die hard, and they'd not always lived in places like this.

Gert grabbed the nearest clothes – the jumper and a pair of leggings she used for dance classes – and threw them on, moving fast and quiet. She fished under the bed on her side and came up with a golf club, shouldered it, and crept to the door.

She waited there, listening, her breathing steady. Sometimes old troubles don't stay where they should. And even pretty little villages aren't immune to new trouble. Especially not this one. She shifted her grip on the club and eased into the hall. Another clatter and the sound of muted movement, someone trying to be quiet. They were in the living room.

Her feet careful on the worn carpet, Gert edged down the hall. The intruder had pulled the living room door to, the dark wood hiding whatever nefarious deeds they were up to. Stealing the presents piled under the tree, maybe. She'd give them what for. And if they weren't just after the presents, but were up to something even worse, well, then she'd give them what for *and* call her favourite grandchild's mum – again, not that she had a favourite grandchild, but if she did, that would be the one whose mum she'd call. There was a woman carrying on the family tradition. She'd know exactly what to do with people who invaded homes and caused mischief. They wouldn't be doing it again.

Gert pressed herself against the wall next to the living room door, a big woman made bigger by the oversized jumper, the sleeves pushed up over the flexed muscle of her forearms and her greying hair hanging damp and lank around her face. She couldn't hear much beyond the door. They were keeping their voices down, although she heard someone hiss, in frustration or triumph, and someone else giggled in an oddly high-pitched tone. More than one, then. She gave a little hiss herself, grabbed the door handle, and charged, bellowing in wordless outrage.

She swung the golf club as she went, keeping it at just the right height to connect with the head of someone who ducked and the belly of someone who didn't, shouting *"Out! Get OUT, you—"*

She cut herself off with a squawk as the golf club hit nothing at all, and the momentum turned her charge into a stumbling spin. She went with it, turning on the spot and dropping to a crouch as she braced herself for an attack. Someone dived for the living room and she bounced up and swung again, catching them a glancing blow to the backside as they scrambled for the cover of the table. She lunged forward, club coming up for another swing, and spotted the open door of the china cabinet a moment too late. She smacked the wooden frame with her nose, hard enough to make her yelp, and bounced away from it, dropping the golf club as she stumbled to her knees.

"Stop!" the intruder shouted. "Gertie, stop!"

"I'll break your bloody neck!" she shouted back, abandoning the club and scrambling after him on all fours, her eyes tearing up from the pain in her nose. "You just wait till I catch you!"

"Stop!" the intruder yelled again, scuttling around the table on hands and knees with Gert in heated pursuit. "Wait!"

"You'll be waiting in a hole in the ground!" She lunged for his feet, grabbing hold of one. He jerked away with a squawk and her fingers slid off his sock. She vaguely thought that it was considerate of home invaders to take their shoes off.

The intruder had made it all the way around the table, and scrambled to his feet as he ran for the living room, still shouting at her to wait. Gert launched herself after him with a furious shout, and he yelped, spinning to meet her with his hands raised. She gave her own startled cry as they collided, falling onto the squat old coffee table together. Gert rolled over the intruder and wound up on the floor between the table and the sofa, while he bounced off her into the cushions and lay there panting wildly.

"Murph?" she demanded from the floor.

"Jesus, Gert, I did try— *watch out!*" He flailed wildly, trying to pull himself out of the sofa as the Christmas tree pitched toward them. Gert covered her face with a squeak, and Murph rolled on top of her just before the tree hit the table.

All Gert could hear was her own ragged breathing and his, a rough chorus. Some branches were sticking into her legs, and Murph had an elbow jammed into her ribs, but nothing seemed to be broken. Not that the same could probably be said of the tree by this point.

"What're you *playing* at?" she demanded. "I almost brained you!"

"I noticed," he said, trying to push himself off. "Ow."

"Why're you even home?"

"I do live here," he said. "And I just saved you from a tree!"

"*Saved* me from it? It wouldn't have fallen over if you hadn't been playing silly beggars!"

"I wasn't! I just – I just needed to get something!"

"You were sneaking about!"

"I was not!" Murph insisted, and they glared at each other from very close quarters for a moment until a giggle floated to them from the tree. Gert blinked. Murph looked anywhere but at her.

"What the hell was that?" she asked.

"I didn't hear anything," Murph said, without much conviction.

"Someone giggled." It came again, and this time it was answered by a chorus of even more delighted snickering. "There!"

"I'm sure I don't know what you mean," he said, and began to thrash about like a landed fish. "I'm stuck!"

"Calm down. Just push the table away. Are you sure you didn't hear anything?"

"There's nothing to hear," he said, and threw his weight against the table.

Gert frowned. If he couldn't hear it, that meant the giggles belonged to something distinctly Toot Hansell-ish, and it also meant she needed to make sure he didn't *start* hearing things. That could lead to seeing things, and the last thing she needed to be doing was trying to explain dragons. That was W.I. business, and husbands just weren't equipped to handle that sort of thing. She put one hand against the sofa and the other against the table, and *pushed*.

The table slid grudgingly away, leaving tracks in the carpet, and the tree collapsed sadly on top of Gert as Murph rolled off her.

"Ow," she said, as a branch tried to stick her in the eye. "Give us a hand here, would you?"

"One moment." Murph scrambled away, scuffling on the other side of the table.

"*Murph!* Help me move this bloody tree!"

"Just a sec, love." There was a thump, a hiss, and Murph swore.

"Murph? What's going on?"

"Be right there," he called, his voice a little strange, and Gert bucked, kicking the tree and shoving it up high enough that she could start to wriggle out. She clawed her way over the table, the tree still trying to trap her legs, spotted Murph crouched on the floor on the far side, and was about to ask him what the hell he was playing at when she saw the red-clad figure of the elf. It was standing in the middle of the floor and giving what were unmistakably *come try me if you think you're hard enough* waves. Gert blinked at it. Murph flung himself forward, grabbing the elf with both hands and bellyflopping to the floor, and seven china milk-maids broke cover from various hiding places, waving the forks she'd put out for the W.I. and shrieking in fury. The eighth was standing by the curtains with the matchbox from the hearth. A pile of spent matches lay at her feet and the cloth was starting to smoulder.

Murph shrieked when he spotted the milkmaids, struggling to get to his feet without letting go of the elf. Gert kicked her way out from under the tree and rolled across the table, sending a milk-maid staggering back in fright. Then the china figurine regrouped and stabbed at Gert's bare foot with the fork. Gert yelped and kicked her, sending her into the TV cabinet with a rather final crunch.

"Ooh," she whispered to herself, but only had the tiniest moment to feel guilty, because two more were coming at her with forks, and one of them stabbed her ankle rather painfully before she jumped away. "Stop that!" she shouted, and kicked a second one. The third retreated, waving her fork threateningly. The others had reached Murph, forks raised as they rushed at his face, and he let go of the elf, rearing to his knees and out of their reach. The milkmaids went for his knees instead, making him squawk, and the elf snatched a fork off one and pushed her away as he joined the attack.

Gert jumped over the nearest milkmaid and ran for the golf club, snatching it up with the little china figure in hot pursuit. She smacked her at close range, sending the maid flying across the room, then turned in time to see the elf running toward her with the fork raised.

"I never liked you anyway," she told him, and swung the club. The elf jumped as the club sailed toward him, leaping over the head and catching hold of the handle, sliding down its length toward her as it finished its arc above her shoulder. She swung again, and his expression went from delight to alarm as he abruptly reversed direction. He shot down the handle, slid over the head of the club and shot off the end with a screech. He hit the wall and slid back down, and before he could sit up Murph flopped himself across the floor, grabbed the elf, and shoved him into a biscuit tin that had been sitting on the coffee table. He slammed the lid on and fell onto his back, panting. There was a fork sticking out of his thigh, and the remains of china milkmaids were scattered across the carpet. The lone survivor looked from him to Gert, hesitating, and Gert swung the golf club in one final arc, sending the milkmaid into the hearth with a pleasing crunch.

Then there was silence but for the hammer of tiny fists on the biscuit tin lid, and some muffled screaming. Murph clutched the tin a bit tighter, staring at the ceiling. His glasses were hanging off one ear and there were scraps of tinsel in the last of his hair.

Gert looked at the golf club and tapped it off the floor a few times, regarding the china birds in the cabinet suspiciously. They didn't seem to have moved.

"I'm so sorry," Murph said to the ceiling. "I thought I got rid of him after the alpine thing."

"You said that was the cats."

"It sounded more plausible." He turned his head to look at her. "He wasn't even that bad back then. Just a bit … mischievous. Certainly not corrupting innocent china milkmaids."

Gert touched her nose. It still smarted from running into the cabinet, but there didn't seem to be any blood. "Why didn't you tell me?"

"Well. It sounds a bit silly, doesn't it? 'The elf's coming to life and getting into the brandy'? You'd have thought I was going dotty."

"Huh. So that's what happened to all the brandy. I thought you were sneaking it out to your boys' club at the allotment."

He shook his head. "It was him. And I think he was getting the hedgehogs drunk. I kept finding them wandering around the garden in the day, and they couldn't walk a straight line between them. But after he trashed the alpine set-up – it looked like he had some sort of party, to be honest, you didn't see the half of it – I took him to the allotment and buried him with the turnips. When you found him this morning … well, I knew I had to get rid of him before he made any more trouble."

"You could've told me," Gert said, and waved at the devastated living room. "Might've been easier."

He frowned at her. "You're taking the whole degenerate Christmas elf thing rather well."

"I suppose." She thought of dragons, then dismissed it. She and Murph had always known the value of not asking too many questions about certain aspects of each other's lives. It had stood them in good stead in the old days, and it would here, too. "I'm just open-minded." She went to the sideboard and fished out the whisky, slopping a generous amount into two of the cups she'd set out for the W.I. She held one out to him, and he pushed himself into a sitting position, careful not to ease his grip on the biscuit tin.

"This open-minded, though?" he asked, taking the cup.

"It seems so," Gert said, sipping the whisky.

They stared at each other, then Murph raised his glass in a silent toast. They both smiled, and in that moment they heard the unmistakable sound of the kitchen door opening.

"Hello?" Miriam shouted. "It's just us! We're early."

Murph gave Gert a horrified look. "I forgot to lock it."

She just shrugged and called, "In here, Miriam."

There was the clatter of tins and Tupperware being dropped on the kitchen table, and the scuffle of jackets being pulled off, then Miriam put her head around the door. "I hope we're not too early. I brought some soup that needs warming up, and Alice and I wanted to talk to you before anyone else arrived anyway, and— Ooh." She stared at Murph, sitting amid the debris of the room, at the fallen tree and scraps of milkmaid everywhere, then back at Gert, her eyes wide. Alice peered around her. No one spoke.

Finally Alice said, "Hello, Murphy. Lovely to see you. Gert, dear, do you know your curtains are on fire?"

"Bollocks," Murph said faintly.

YORKSHIRE PUDDINGS

Right, we've already established that I was worried about creating a cross-border incident by renaming Welsh rarebit, and now I get to confess that a New Zealander offering up a Yorkshire pudding recipe is probably Not The Done Thing.

Yorkshire puddings are a bit of a source of pride around here, with everyone having their own recipe (often with secret techniques and/or ingredients to guarantee success), and everyone's mum making undoubtedly *the best* Yorkshire puddings in existence, and non-Yorkshire TV chefs being regularly scoffed at for daring to offer their own versions. I sort of feel coming in here having only discovered Yorkshire puds in the last fifteen years or so, that even having an opinion on them may be dangerous.

However, I offer in my defence that the SO is both a chef and thoroughly Yorkshire, and I learned to make them from another Yorkshireman who does make excellent puds. So I will pass all responsibility and credit on to them.

Yorkshire puddings as we know them are delightfully light, fluffy concoctions that blossom out of hot oil in the oven and are a non-negotiable aspect of the Sunday roast dinner. They appear in the record around the same time as Welsh rarebit, in the first half of the eighteenth century, but the pudding itself had been around for centuries in the form of "dripping pudding", so named because it was made in the dripping collected from a roast dinner. It started off as a cheap way to fill hungry tummies, a mix of flour, eggs, and milk that was served with thick gravy and eaten first, so the meat of the main course would go further. Of course, not everyone was lucky enough to have meat for the main course, so the pudding could also be the entire meal.

The original dripping puddings never rose much. However, these days we expect better. According to The Royal Society of Chemistry, "A Yorkshire pudding isn't a Yorkshire pudding if it is less than four inches tall." Which is both the trick and the delight of Yorkshire puds, and why everybody has their own secret recipe.

All this lovely rise means you'll get a nice well inside most puds. This is ideal not just for flooding with gravy on a plate, but also for stuffing with roast beef and horseradish cream, or sautéed mushrooms and spinach, or any number of lovely things and eating as nibbles. The Yorkshireman who originally taught me how to make them used to use half for the roast dinner and the other half for a starter of what he called "Yorkshire salad" – a mix of sliced iceberg lettuce, vinegar, and sugar which was weirdly good.

If you are stuffing them to use as nibbles, keep the fillings fairly dry and provide lots of napkins. They're not elegant. But they are delicious.

- 140 g / a little less than 1 cup flour
- 4 eggs
- 200 mL / 1 cup less 1 Tbsp milk
- oil

Whisk the flour, eggs and milk in a measuring jug until well-combined and no lumps remain, then let it rest. You can do this in the morning and ignore it until you're ready to cook.

When you're ready, pop the oven to 230°C / just under 450°F. Pour enough oil into the bottoms of two 12-muffin pans to cover them generously. Pop the trays in the oven and let them heat.

When the oil is completely up to heat, *carefully* remove one tray from the oven. Really carefully. I cannot stress this enough. Immediately pour a small amount of batter into each muffin well – the batter plus oil shouldn't come more than a quarter of the way up the pan.

Carefully return the tray to the oven and repeat with the second tray – you'll get around 20 from this mix. Bake for 20–25 minutes, or until the puddings are well-browned and beautifully puffed.

Remove from oven and immediately roll the puddings upside down, so any oil inside drains away and they're not sitting in the wells of the tray anymore. Eat immediately, or set aside and reheat just long enough to crisp up again when needed. They also freeze very well.

9

NINE LADIES DANCING

Miriam thought that, one day, she might be able to say "no" when someone asked her something. Not something simple, like if she'd like another cup of tea or piece of cake (although, to be fair, she rarely *wanted* to say no to such things, so she didn't exercise her no muscle there very much), but more serious somethings. Like getting tangled up in investigations, for instance, not that anyone ever really *asked* her about that. Or being a designated driver for a W.I. night out (it was the driving bit, not the designated bit, that worried her). Or doing a walk-a-thon with Teresa, when she felt her own abilities lay rather more in the bake-a-thon arena.

Or learning a dance routine for the Christmas market opening night, where they already had a stall and plenty to do to get ready for that. She tugged her orange jumper down a bit. She was sure it was making her look remarkably like a pumpkin, and her dance abilities were at about the same level. She scowled at Alice, who was sitting on a folding chair in the village hall, watching the nine women on the stage and resolutely not smiling, although Miriam saw her lips twitch more than once.

She scrambled down off the stage and went to sit next to Alice, puffing a bit. Alice handed her a glass of water, and she gulped it down.

"This is ridiculous," she announced.

"It's for charity," Alice said, watching Jasmine do some fancy in-and-out foot thing. Gert copied her flawlessly. Rosemary and Carlotta started off on opposite feet and bumped into each other, setting Priya giggling, and Rose was apparently tap-dancing to a different song entirely on the edge of the stage.

"I don't see you doing it," Miriam said.

"I have a bad hip."

"That doesn't stop you chasing criminals about the place, does it?" Miriam demanded, and peeled her jumper off. She was *far* too hot, and she couldn't tell if it was the hall heating playing up, the dancing, or a hot flush, which was a misnomer if ever she heard one. It was more like a volcanic flood.

Alice gave her an amused look. "I suppose I'm saving myself in case of criminal foot pursuits, then."

Miriam puffed air over her top lip. "You cheat."

"Oh, no," Alice said. "It's just strategic avoidance." And she handed Miriam a florentine.

"You can't buy me off," Miriam said, but she took the biscuit anyway. Alice made rather excellent florentines.

IT WAS mid-afternoon by the time Jasmine let them stop, and that was only because Rose sat down in the middle of the stage and refused to move.

"But the opening night's *tomorrow*," Jasmine said. "We have to be ready!"

"We're as ready as we can be," Pearl said. "We're not going to turn into the Royal Academy in the next few hours."

"Besides, we need a little time to finish off everything for the stall," Carlotta said. "I'm still catching up on the amaretti after that horrible bird destroyed everything."

Jasmine crossed her arms over her chest and frowned at the women. She was wearing a singlet with very excitable writing on the front, and bright yellow trainers. Everyone else had turned up in whatever they had, which in Miriam's case was flip-flops, and they were causing her no end of trouble.

"You're not taking this seriously," Jasmine announced. "Just because it's something different. Why can't we try something other than baking and wreaths?"

"My legs are taking it very seriously," Rosemary said, from where she'd joined Rose on the floor. "I won't even be able to stand up tomorrow, let alone dance."

"One more," Jasmine pleaded. "We'll just run through the whole song one more time, then we'll be done."

The ladies of the Toot Hansell Women's Institute looked at each other, and Miriam sighed, taking up her position behind Priya and Rose. At least no one was having to find a polite way to ask Jasmine not to make anything for the market stall, or not to make wreaths, or, in fact, not to even make mulled wine. Miriam raised her arms as the song started, wondering how one made a mess of mulled wine. It was alcohol and spices, yet somehow Jasmine's always had a faint green tinge and tasted of stale onions. It was most odd. She spun in the wrong direction, bumped into Pearl, rebounded, tripped over Carlotta's outstretched leg, and gave Jasmine an apologetic smile.

That was what one got for thinking about mulled wine while dancing, she supposed.

MARKET MORNING WAS ALWAYS A RUSH, and the Christmas market even more so. They'd come down the night before to wrap wreaths around the frame inside the stall and to set up the folding tables, Rose shouting that they needed more light at the startled council workers who were running extension cables under protective covers to stop people tripping on them. Other stalls had been setting up too, vans crowding around the little square and people hurrying back and forth with armfuls of paper cups and napkins and lights and tablecloths and urns and all the other accoutrements of commerce.

But even with all that done last night, there was still the stock to carry in before they opened at ten, and Miriam hadn't even finished breakfast when she opened her front door and waved at Gert, who had pulled to the kerb in a squat white van. Miriam kicked into her clogs and took the first of the boxes of mince pies out as Rose clambered out of the cab to help her.

"Don't you get crumbs everywhere," Gert said, as, loading done, Miriam climbed in next to Rose with a piece of toast in one hand. "This is my nephew's cousin's daughter's van."

"How lovely," Miriam said around a mouthful of toast, wrinkling her nose and looking at Rose. Rose nodded. The van smelled distinctly of fish.

They did the rounds of all the W.I. houses, collecting chocolate florentines and Christmas shortbread, brandy snaps and the heavy, fragrant rounds of fruitcake and more mince pies, and before long Miriam could smell more spice and less fish. Although not *entirely* no fish, which wasn't ideal. They trundled carefully through the quiet streets of Toot Hansell, the Christmas lights of the houses spilling the promise of magic, and she almost forgot about the dancing.

Almost.

By the time the market opened at ten the W.I. stall was overflowing with cake and biscuits, and scattered with little blackboard signs neatly printed with prices. Lights twinkled among the wreathes that swathed the stall, and Mortimer's magical dragon scale baubles floated above it, tethered with string and glowing from within, and the air smelled of hot chocolate and mulled wine and, somewhere in the distance, the cool, crisp promise of snow.

Alice stood back from the stall, surveying everything, and nodded in satisfaction. "That will do quite nicely," she said, and adjusted a sign on the hot chocolate urn minutely.

"Here we go," Priya said, and snuggled herself more securely into her coat as the first of the shoppers started to filter through the aisles of the stalls.

It was busy – not as busy as Friday and Saturday would be, of course, but before lunch they'd already had to refill the hot water urn for the tea twice, and the mulled wine once, which seemed like it was starting very early, but, as every person who bought it pointed out, it *was* almost Christmas. The ladies of the W.I. took turns in the stall, someone restocking the pretty jars and tins of gift biscuits and cake, and replenishing the plates of sliced fruit cake and minced pies while two others served. The rest took the chance to go home and warm up, or to explore the rest of the stalls. Not, Miriam thought, as she bought a rather luxuriant scarf which she thought Beaufort might prefer to his flat cap, that they had anything like the lovely food of the W.I. stall on offer. But if one wanted a bacon butty or some venison sausages there were some rather nice ones to be had.

The market also seemed reassuringly *human*. Miriam wasn't quite sure what she'd expected, but after the sprite's talk of magic spills and the dragons worrying about things getting worse, she'd half-expected that by the time the day was out they'd be being mobbed by geese or swearing lizards or Christmas elves or something she hadn't even thought of yet. Everyone knew to look out for anything *odd*, but there was nothing stranger than a busker singing Christmas songs in a Hawaiian shirt, with a large fake parrot stuck to one shoulder. The rest were families and couples and little groups of friends, running from stall to stall and collecting bags and boxes to go with their pink noses and sticky fingers. Even the big Christmas tree, towering over the stalls, appeared to be uninhabited. She did keep checking on it, though. It was making her faintly nervous.

By the end of the afternoon they'd sold out of nearly everything they'd brought with them, and half the W.I. were at home rolling out more mince pies and biscuits for the next day. Gert was making more mulled wine, which Miriam wasn't sure about. Two customers had already come back with streaming eyes to ask if they could have a little hot water to dilute it, and she rather disagreed with Gert's verdict that they were just lightweights. The fumes were enough to make her tipsy.

"Ooh, it has been busy," Jasmine said, holding her hands over the little heater under the counter. "I hope everyone's not too tired for the recital."

Miriam made a small, despairing noise. She'd somehow managed to forget that tonight they were going to have to stand in front of the whole village and dance to a song called "Happy", which was exactly the opposite of how the idea made her feel.

"Well, I hope Mortimer has more baubles," Alice said, wedging some more money into the overstuffed cash box. "We've almost sold out."

Miriam looked up at the dragon scale baubles, lit from within and brightening the dark sky. Mortimer had been working on a snowflake theme this year, and they were delicate and intricate and utterly individual. They were snuggled down into the garlands now, she noticed. They looked rather nice, although it was always good to show off how they floated in the air, like stars come to rest.

"Miriam?" Jasmine said.

"I'm sorry?" Miriam had the idea that Jasmine had asked her something, but she'd been too busy looking at the baubles.

"I said, do you have your outfit with you?"

"My outfit?"

"For the dance." Jasmine folded her arms over her chest. "Don't tell me you left it at home. You'll have to go and get it now – you'll be late otherwise!"

"That *would* be a shame," Miriam said, and Alice gave a ladylike cough that sounded an awful lot like she was covering up a very unladylike snort.

"Go and get it now," Jasmine ordered. "Honestly! Why are you all being so difficult?"

Miriam hurried out of the stall, her ears burning, and as she trotted away she heard Alice say, "You'll get used to it, dear."

MIRIAM WAS ACTUALLY GOING to be late. She hadn't *meant* to be, but by the time she'd walked home and thrown on the red jumper and black leggings that constituted her outfit (finished off with a woolly hat and her big warm boots, because it wasn't as if the shoes were the problem with her dancing), and given herself five minutes to shuffle around the kitchen as she tried to remember the steps, she'd decided she'd be best to drive back. But her old VW Beetle just whined when she turned the key, and after losing precious time alternately coaxing and shouting, she jumped out and set off for the market at a jog.

The jog only lasted a couple of blocks before she had to slow down and strip off her coat and hat, fanning herself as she stumbled on into town. She was going to arrive completely drenched in sweat and feeling awful, as well as late. "Sorry, Jasmine," she mumbled, and as soon as she'd cooled down she picked up her pace again. It wasn't far. Perhaps she could sneak in at the back of the group.

By the time she got to the market most of the stalls were closed, canvas fronts strapped firmly down and lights switched off, and the only noise of people she could hear came from the centre of the market, where the little stage was set up by the well, and where she should most certainly be by now.

"Oh no," she whispered, and tried to go a bit faster, hurrying down the lanes between the stalls. The cobbles crunched with grit underfoot, and the lights strung above the square gave everything a magical glow. She glanced toward the W.I. stall as she passed, checking everyone was actually gone, and staggered to a halt. The stall ... the stall *should* have been there. Or it was there, but ... Miriam took an uncertain step forward, dance forgotten, just as Rose raced past her waving an axe.

"Rose?" she shouted.

"Oi! You haven't paid for that!" The man from the shop that sold everything from wooden spoons to fancy toilets ran after Rose. "You can't just *take* it!"

Rose shouted something wordless and hefted the axe like a diminutive Viking, launching herself at the stall. A garland promptly dropped from the nearest lamp post and snaked around the axe, dragging Rose into the air as it retreated. Rose clung on grimly, swearing at the garland, and only let go when it gave the axe an impatient shake.

"What the *hell?*" the shopkeeper asked, which was pretty much Miriam's thought too, but she just grabbed his arm and said, "It's rehearsal."

"Rehearsal for what?" he asked, craning to look up the lamp post. "That's my axe, that is!"

"We'll be in to pay later," Miriam said, giving him her most reassuring grin. He didn't look very reassured, so she added, "Cold out here, isn't it?"

The man looked down at himself, as if only just noticing he was wearing a T-shirt, and shivered. "Alright. But I know who you are, so you better pay!"

"We will," Miriam said, and rushed to Rose as the man retreated. "Rose! Are you okay?"

The older woman squinted up at the garland, and shook a small fist at it. "I've got a chainsaw at home with your name on it, buddy."

The garland gave a theatrical shiver, and Miriam tried not to imagine Rose let loose with a chainsaw. "What's going on? What's happened to the stall?"

They turned to look at what appeared to be a very large, very healthy holly bush, occupying the exact spot the stall had been when Miriam went home to get changed. It was sporting some randomly placed ribbons and pine branches, and Mortimer's baubles glimmered deep amongst the greenery.

"They're all in there," Rose said. "How do we get them out?"

Miriam crept a little closer and tried tugging at a smaller branch. It jerked away from her, stabbing her with sharp-edged leaves as it did so. "Ow! Not like that, then."

"And not with an axe, either, it appears." Rose tapped her fingers on her chin. "Fire brigade?"

"And tell them our friends are trapped in a hedge?"

Rose nodded. "Yes, they may not treat it with the urgency it requires."

Miriam sighed. "We really need to set up a way to get hold of the dragons." They both stared at the bush, then Miriam shouted, "Alice? Are you okay?"

A muffled shout came back to them, although they couldn't quite make out the words.

"Well, at least it hasn't eaten them," Rose said.

"It's only holly," Miriam pointed out.

"That has eaten the entire stall."

"Well, fair." They both looked at the stall for a moment longer, and Miriam thought of the dragons huddled by the fishpond with the rain slick on their scales. Belief, they'd said. Too much belief. She dug in her coat pocket and found a small bottle of hand sanitiser she'd been using in the stall. Well, it couldn't hurt. "It's a good thing you picked up that weedkiller," she said to Rose.

"What?"

Miriam flipped the cap open. "When you got the axe. You picked up this weedkiller that kills" – she checked the label – "… 99% of … weeds."

The holly gave a startled tremble.

"You only need a few drops," Miriam read. "A little goes a long way."

The garland slunk down off the lamp post, still clutching the axe. Rose was staring at Miriam as if she'd gone dotty, but Miriam just waved the little bottle threateningly at the stall.

"Don't make me use this!"

There was silence for a moment, and Miriam was aware of a whisper in the leaves, something not human or Folk, but old and endless and maybe a little confused. Then there was a crash from the heart of the holly and a hand wielding a breadknife popped through.

"Get a damn chainsaw!" Gert bellowed, pushing her face against the gap. "It's gaining on us in here!"

"Weedkiller!" Miriam shouted. "Use the weedkiller!"

"You *what?*" Gert demanded, then gave a yelp and vanished from view, fighting to keep hold of the breadknife.

"*Weedkiller!*" Miriam shouted again, and squirted a few drops of sanitiser at a wreath that was tiptoeing toward them. It reversed rapidly, and Rose stared at her.

"Weedkiller," Rose said, then more loudly, "Alcohol! The mulled wine! *Gert, the urns!*"

There was more shouting from inside, and Miriam advanced on the holly as Rose fished in her jacket and came up with a hip flask. Miriam raised her eyebrows.

"What?" Rose said. "It's damn cold out here."

The garland made a clumsy swing at them with the axe, and they both shrieked and splashed it with a heady mix of sanitiser and alcohol. The garland dropped the axe and shot up to the top of the lamp post, where it curled into a ball and quivered.

"Yeah!" Rose shouted. "And stay there!"

The shouting inside the stall was louder now, as if the foliage were thinning, and Miriam waved the hand sanitiser, setting the leaves hissing against each other as they shook.

"Let them go!" she shouted. "Let them go *now!*"

"Take that!" Rose shouted next to her, and threw a stinging arc of brandy through the air just as Teresa tore a gap in the branches and shoved her head through.

"Ow!"

"Duck," Rose said, rather belatedly, and the scent of spilled mulled wine, rather on the over-fortified side, rolled out of the stall as the holly started to slink away, lights re-merging as the cover thinned. Wreaths crawled back to their places and garlands tried to look innocent, and Priya was throwing mulled wine in every direction while Pearl tried to keep behind her. Rosemary and Carlotta stood back to back, hacking at the undergrowth with scissors. Gert was still wielding the breadknife with utter abandon, and Jasmine was hammering at a shrinking wreath with an empty thermos, while Alice stood in the middle of it all with her hat uncharacteristically askew and a jug of mulled wine in each hand. The heater was sparking rather violently, and she leaned over to switch it off.

The last garland caterpillared past Miriam's feet as it retreated to the stall next door, and she had the idea that it was whimpering. She looked at the hand sanitiser and tried not to feel *too* guilty.

"Well," Alice said. "That was exciting."

"That was uncalled for," Gert said, plucking some holly out of her hair.

"We're going to have to clean this up before we leave," Rosemary said, and the W.I. stared at the stall, cluttered with dislodged cups and dropped plates and shed leaves, napkins papering the floor and walls like an explosion of dishevelled petals, and the whole thing dripping with red wine and bits of orange and cinnamon sticks.

"Oh dear," Carlotta said. "Can we just get a hose …?"

"That might be how you do it in Manchester," Rosemary started, and Jasmine interrupted her.

"The recital! We're late!"

"We just got attacked by the decorations," Priya said. "Doesn't that give us a pass?"

"*No,*" Jasmine said firmly, and when no one said anything, she added, "It's for charity!"

The ladies looked at each other doubtfully, then Alice dropped the empty jugs on one of the tables. "Come on," she said. "Hurry! We can still make it!"

"Really?" Miriam asked weakly, but she ran after the nine other ladies of the Toot Hansell Women's Institute as they charged down the aisles of stalls into the square at the heart of the market, abandoning the wine-slicked chaos of their own stall behind them. Alice grabbed their jackets as Jasmine led them on stage, and they lined up, with scratches on their hands and twigs in their hair, as the butcher's son started the song playing, and the music rang off the tents. Miriam put her hands in the air, took a deep breath, and twirled, in the right direction this time, seeing Alice clapping merrily and smiling up at them, and hearing Pearl giggling as she got the hand movements wrong, and Rose humming to herself in an entirely different tune, and she thought, *happy.* Well. Maybe.

Above them the stars glimmered around the top of the tree, and below them the crowd cheered and clapped and stomped their feet, and entirely drowned out the woman off to the side of the stage who was saying rather loudly to her friend, "Look at the *state* of them. And the smell! They must've come straight from the pub."

MULLED APPLE JUICE

It's *kind* of annoying being a non-drinker around the holiday period. Well, not everywhere. Just at Christmas markets, for the most part. While every second stall seems to sell mulled wine, the only other option tends to be hot chocolate, which, while lovely, is often too sweet for a nice little afternoon drink to wander about with. And yes, I could have tea, but tea served in a paper cup from a market stall is very rarely at the same level as the nice cuppa you make at home using a teapot and your favourite mug.

Which means that the rare times I stumble onto a stall selling spiced apple juice, I am *delighted*. It's an easy, warming drink that makes you feel suitably festive, isn't so sweet that you can't have a piece of cake with it, and basically feels like enough of a treat that not even the most reluctant designated driver can feel left out.

So I decided to give you the recipe for that instead of mulled wine, although when confronted with aggressive greenery I'd probably stick with the alcohol.

- 1 L / 2 pints apple juice (I prefer cloudy)
- 4 or 5 slices of fresh ginger

- 2 cinnamon sticks
- 2 star anise
- 4 cloves
- a generous grating of nutmeg
- several strips of orange zest

Combine all of the above in a saucepan and heat until steaming gently. Keep it warm as is, and sieve to order, or give it at least 10 minutes before sieving and serving.

That's it! You can of course adjust the spices to suit your personal tastes. I won't be upset.

10

TEN LORDS A-LEAPING

Mortimer rushed into the Grand Cavern, his wings steaming as he hit the combined heat of the fire that always burned in the centre of the big cave, and the body heat of a whole brew of dragons. He paused, frowning and blinking away the condensation that was running off his scales into his eyes. He'd been hoping to talk to Beaufort alone, but there were an awful lot of dragons in here today. There were always a few, but not usually this many. All dragons had their own caverns, sometimes shared, sometimes not, and while dragons enjoy a little social time as much as any other creature, it seemed *everyone* had decided to be social at once today. He wondered how many of them could feel that same unease seeping up from the village, magic in the air like a mirage on hot earth.

He padded through the crowd, quite a few of whom were sporting woolly hats, tail warmers, and, in the case of Wendy, a sort of shawl that was bunched up between her wings. She looked both far too hot and a little smug, and two small dragons were crouched behind her, working on unravelling one corner with quiet determination.

Beaufort's big barbecue, sitting on the outcropping which had once held a rather more traditional nest of old swords and broken shields, was empty, but the High Lord was sitting next to it, his front paws folded over his belly while he listened to a sleek she-fox with an elegant brush and quick keen eyes.

"I tell you," she was saying as Mortimer sat down to wait nearby, "it's not just gnomes. Some damn *elves* started getting all up in my tail with their flutes and lutes and nonsense. Right by our den! No one needs that. It brings the neighbourhood right down, it does."

"You're quite right," Beaufort said, nodding. "Terribly troublesome, elves. All that frolicking. And poetry."

"*Poetry*," the she-fox agreed. "And then they get all overcome and start sighing about the place. It's not good for the more impressionable youngsters."

"Well, we'll have words with them," Beaufort said. "I'm sure there must be more suitable places for poetry."

"I'm not sure anywhere's really suitable for poetry," the she-fox said, and trotted off.

Beaufort watched her go, then gave Mortimer a toothy grin. "Hello, lad. Tell me you're not coming to complain, too. Everyone's complaining about everyone else at the moment – even more so than usual."

"Um," Mortimer said, then handed Beaufort the tin he'd had tucked under his foreleg. "Mince pie?"

"Wonderful." The High Lord took the tin and prised the lid off carefully. "Have you and Amelia been to take more baubles down to Miriam, then?"

"Yes, we just dropped them off." He took a breath. Well, it wasn't complaining *exactly*, was it? Just stating the facts. "Um, sir, something really weird happened to them at the market last night."

"Let me guess," Beaufort said, selecting a mince pie. "The trees?"

"Yes! They were *attacked* by garlands! And all the wreaths had axes, and Miriam had to fight them with hand soap!" Now he said it, he wondered if Miriam had been exaggerating a tiny wee bit. He wasn't sure where the wreaths had got all these axes from.

Beaufort sighed. "I was worried something like this might happen. I had the dryads in here only yesterday complaining that the humans were taking their trees and branches without so much as a thank you, and saying they wanted something done about it."

"But they already attacked that man with snapping turtles."

"It's possible that they felt no one had learned their lesson." Beaufort offered Mortimer the tin, and he took a mince pie, even though he'd already had at least six at Miriam's. This situation called for multiple mince pies, he felt.

"Is it the magic spill?" he asked.

"I rather think so," Beaufort said. "Everyone seems to be very heated about everything. The brownies are insisting they want to restart the old practise of cursing households. Lydia says she found a faery circle on the edge of the woods and had to dig it all up so no one got trapped. And Nellie from the duck pond swears she saw a Nessie in the tarn."

"*Our* tarn?"

"Yes. Tell Gilbert not to feed it, would you? We'll never get rid of it if he does."

"We've had dwarves around, too," Mortimer said. "They sent a deputation requesting we set up a meeting with the village council to allow them to sell their goods at the market, since we were selling baubles."

"Oh dear," Beaufort said. "What did you tell them?"

"I got Amelia to talk to them."

"Ah. Well, that'll be settled, then," Beaufort said, and set the tin down to shake his wings out. "Not too long until Christmas, and then this will all calm down." His voice was rougher than usual, and Mortimer could see a couple of scales on his tail that were looking a little dull.

He took a breath, and tried to ignore the High Lord's dull scales. After all, he'd shed three scales this morning already. "What if it doesn't?"

Beaufort looked at him, not speaking.

"What if this is just the start? What if things just keep getting worse? How do we fix it?"

Beaufort waited.

Mortimer looked at his paws. "We've done this, haven't we? By spending time in the village? We've … changed something. We've made it easier, or more possible, or *something* for all the other Folk to show themselves."

Still silence from the old dragon, while he watched Mortimer with eyes that had seen centuries rise and fall, alliances fracture and blossom and collapse again.

"It's our fault," Mortimer said. "We … we broke the balance."

"You bloody well did," a new voice said, sounding like boulders moving in a flood. "And *this* is what messing around with the bloody Women's Institute and fancying yourselves detectives gets you." Lord Walter shuffled up and glared at them both through milky eyes. "We'll have the damn Watch down on us by the new year, you mark my words."

"They *wouldn't*," Mortimer whispered. The Watch, the council which enforced the separation of human and Folk worlds, weren't the sort of cats one wanted to cross. Not even if one was a dragon.

"Isn't that going to be a pretty kettle of fish?" Walter said with some satisfaction. "Centuries of dragons being left to self-govern blown apart by you two and your baked goods."

"The Watch aren't going to know about it," Beaufort said. "Thompson's making sure they don't get wind of anything. And even the Watch know that certain villages are just a little more prone to magical spills than others."

"Thompson, eh?" Walter asked, helping himself to a mince pie. Mortimer had to resist the urge to pull the tin away. "Where's he been lately, then? Haven't seen that scruffy little bag of rags for ages."

Mortimer thought that was a bit rich, considering Walter's skin looked like it had been left out in the rain and stretched three sizes too big for his old bones, but he also thought the old dragon had a point. "I haven't seen him either," he said.

Beaufort scratched his chin. "That's a little concerning. If he's moved on, there'll be a replacement at some point, and they may not be quite so accommodating."

"What might they do?" Mortimer asked. "To the ladies, I mean." Because it was one thing the Watch coming after dragons – other than openly declaring war, which would be both messy and unlikely to pass beneath the notice of humans, there was only so much they could do – but there was a lot they could do to humans.

"They'd wipe their memories," Beaufort said, and Walter snorted.

"Those humans have known you too long," he said. "You can't wipe memories that are so well set. They'd have to just break their silly little minds."

"How can you be so *awful?*" someone demanded, and Mortimer looked around at Amelia. Rain was steaming off her and she was a furious puce colour, even deeper and more vibrant than when she'd been arguing with the dwarves. "You sit there scoffing their mince pies and talk about our *friends* like that? And don't think I don't know you go sneaking around Rose's all the time! You're just a horrible hypocritical old toad with tatty wings and—"

"*Amelia!*" Mortimer hissed, as Walter turned to the young dragon with smoke dribbling from his jaws. "Shut up!"

"No! Someone has to tell him! He's such a—"

"Do you know," Walter interrupted, "us old Folk did just fine without you young lot and your *ideals* shouting at us all the time.

We can make up our own minds without being harangued. It's rude and unnecessary and all I was *going* to say is that we'd better get our tails down to that village and make bloody sure the Watch don't find out, hadn't we?"

Amelia stared at him. "Oh," she said.

Beaufort examined Walter. "To be fair, you really could do to get some patches on those wings before they get any worse. I'm sure Mortimer could come up with something."

"What?" Mortimer squeaked.

"My wings are *fine*," Walter snapped, and shook them out clumsily, shedding half a dozen scales and making Amelia duck. "I'm a fine figure of a dragon."

"Of a dead one, maybe," Amelia muttered.

"Eh?" Walter asked, glaring at Mortimer. "What was that?"

"I didn't say anything," he protested, looking to Beaufort for help, but the High Lord was squinting at the cavern entrance, where Gilbert had just scampered in with something cradled in one foreleg. He was dripping wet.

"Oh, no," Mortimer said.

"Look!" Gilbert shouted, hopping toward them. "I found a lake monster!"

"Well, why didn't you leave it in the lake?" Amelia demanded. "It's probably drowning in the air. And you're dripping on the floor! People have to walk on that, you know!"

Gilbert ignored his sister. "Mortimer, look!"

Mortimer looked at Beaufort, who tapped his talons on the floor and looked at Walter. "Are we in agreement, then, Walter?" the High Lord asked.

"On this and *only* this," Walter said. "I still think this befriending humans is foolishness. Accepting offerings is one thing, but *befriending* them? Why, when I were a lad—"

"Morti-*mer*," Gilbert insisted, as Amelia slapped his shoulder.

"Leave Mortimer alone! He's busy!"

Mortimer looked at Gilbert and his bundle, and said, "Um," then Beaufort said his name and he turned away gratefully. "Sir?"

"Are we in agreement, Mortimer?"

"*Me?*"

"Mortimer—" Gilbert tried again, as his bundle grew legs and slid to the floor.

"*Shut up, Gilbert!*" Amelia hissed.

"Stop it you *children!*" Walter bawled at the two young dragons, and Gilbert ducked behind Amelia as the lake monster flopped ungracefully away.

Beaufort ignored them all, still looking at Mortimer. "Do you think this is the best course of action, lad? Do we involve ourselves further, or do we retreat?"

Mortimer could actually feel the last of his colour draining away. "Beaufort, sir, it's not really … I mean, that's really your decision and not mine …"

"You're terribly sensible and know more about humans than any other dragon here," Beaufort said. "So what do you think?"

Mortimer blinked at him, and wondered if he should grab Gilbert's lake monster and run back out into the rain with it. He could sit at the bottom of the tarn until people stopped asking him difficult questions. As if he really knew *anything* about humans! They were just as confusing as dragons. And, fine, the barbecues *had* been his idea, a way of keeping dragons warm without spending all their time hunting for fuel, but had it been worth it? Really? Putting Miriam at risk of attack by irate Christmas wreaths, and the dragons at risk of discovery?

He looked away from Beaufort, at the crowded warmth of the chamber. No one was out hunting for wood. There were spare rabbits piled by the fire for anyone who wanted them. There were barbecues and gas cylinders tucked in all around the dragons' mount, and seven eggs had hatched last spring. Seven!

"It's helped us," he said to Beaufort. "But what about Miriam and the others? Have we helped them? Really?"

"I don't know," the High Lord said. "It depends what you mean by *help*. Friendship isn't quantifiable. It's not like setting up a trade agreement. A friendship would be a terribly cold thing, if that were the case."

Mortimer thought about that, and about drinking tea in warm kitchens, and Alice pretending not to laugh when Gilbert got overexcited about captive chickens, and Gert sneaking Beaufort her alcoholic cordial, and Rose and Amelia arguing over the classification of butterflies, then said, "Well, we can't just not do anything, can we? I mean, at the very least we need to make sure the Watch doesn't get suspicious."

"At the very least," Beaufort said.

"Then we can ask them, can't we?" Mortimer said.

"I think I know what the answer will be."

"Do we accept their answer? Even when we know it's dangerous?"

"You can't answer for someone else. That's just giving an order. Everyone gets to make their own choices, otherwise it's not a friendship anymore." They looked at each other for a moment, then the High Lord asked again, "Are we in agreement, Mortimer?"

"Yes?" he said.

"Excellent." Beaufort got to his feet and faced the chamber. "Lords of the Cloverly," he shouted, and all around the chamber heads turned toward him, male and female alike (because Lord is a non-gendered term for dragons). "The time has come to protect the village as it has ever protected us. Will you join me?"

"Of course," Lord Pamela said from a perch on the wall. "There's no need to be so *dramatic*, Beaufort."

"They have *mince pies*," Lord Stanley said. "Of course we'll help."

"Mince pies aside," Lord Margery said, "we'd hardly let them drown in magic and get wiped out by the Watch, would we? They're *our* humans."

"Save our humans!" a rather portly dragon in a ski cap shouted, and a cheer went up.

"Well, we seem to have a consensus," Beaufort said. "Amelia, please take your brother and his new friend back to the lake before it eats our dinner." Because the little Loch Ness monster had made it to the fire and was gulping down one of the rabbits, eyes wide with effort and long neck bulging as it forced the rabbit down in one piece. Gilbert was remonstrating with it and waving a baked potato hopefully. "Mortimer, if you could ask everyone except the Lords to leave, then come back and join us. We need to make a plan."

"Come *back?* I'm not a Lord!"

"It's only a title," Beaufort said, and ambled off to wake Lord Heidi, who was snoozing on her back next to the fire.

"A *title,*" Lord Walter said. "It means something, that does! And you can't even fight."

"I know," Mortimer said miserably. He was shedding just from the idea of being included with the Lords. He'd be as threadbare as Lord Walter before he even hit 200, let alone whatever terrible age the old dragon had reached.

"In my day," Walter started, and Amelia talked over him.

"You'd be an amazing Lord, though, Mortimer. Stop everyone being so narrow-minded and nasty." She and Walter glared at each other.

Gilbert wandered up, still holding a potato. "What's this about Lords?"

"Mortimer's going to be a Lord," Amelia said.

"I'm not," Mortimer said, as Walter said, *"Ha!"*

"Cool," Gilbert said. "Except, you know, it's an archaic system which falsely confers status on those who adhere to certain societal standards and should be abolished. But cool anyway."

"Oh, shut up and get your Nessie," Amelia said, starting toward the fire. "He's eaten *four* rabbits!"

"He's really hungry," Gilbert said, following her.

Mortimer scuttled away to start clearing the cavern before Walter could say anything else to make him start stress-shedding. Beaufort hadn't actually *said* he'd be a Lord. And no one could seriously think he'd be any good at it. He made nice baubles and sometimes came up with good ideas, was all. Mostly he just tried to stop Beaufort getting carried away. That was it. And Lords were all about fighting and bravery, and the last fight he'd got into, Amelia had had to save him. So, no. He couldn't be a Lord.

"Mortimer," Beaufort called, as the younger dragon ushered out the last of the stragglers. "Come on! We can't start without you."

For one moment Mortimer considered just bolting out into the rain and winging his way straight to Miriam's house, where he could curl up in front of the Aga with a mince pie, a generous dollop of cream, and a mug of tea, then he remembered that she'd be in the market braving the Christmas garlands again. And that unless he did help, there was no telling what Beaufort would come up with. Probably more dog costumes.

So he turned and trotted to the little group of dragons settled by the fire. Lord Margery shuffled around to make space for him, and Lord Pablo offered him a carrot.

"Want one? Gilbert tells me they're better than squirrels."

"Thanks," Mortimer said weakly, and the ten Lords of the Cloverly dragons (or eight Lords, one High Lord, and one going-to-be-a-Lord-one-day-but-not-looking-forward-to-it), leaned together over the old fire that had burned in the cavern for centuries, and plotted how to save their humans.

DRAGON-FRIENDLY MINCEMEAT

Mince pies are an integral part of the UK festive season. They start popping up in stores in October, quietly at first, then multiplying rapidly across the shelves, spawning variations such as iced mince pies, and luxury mince pies, and mince pies with tops, or lattice, or naked, and gluten-free or vegan or in slices or deep-dish or just about anything else you can think of. Come November, most of the papers are running roundups of the best supermarket mince pies, or the best luxury mince pies, or the best budget ones. They are *inescapable.*

And also basically Christmas in a bite, so this seasonal proliferation of pastries has never bothered me. I usually buy some impulsively at some point, then remember that most commercial mince pies are all pastry and very little filling, so I buy mincemeat instead, and make my own.

However, this year I decided to try making the mincemeat itself. It always seemed like a bit of a faff to me, and the idea of being organised enough to make it a year ahead of time (or whatever it is) is somewhat laughable when you're the sort of person who has dinner late most nights because she forgets she has to make it.

But it did seem a little bit of a cheat not to at least try, considering I already make my own pastry. It was a worthwhile experiment, at least. So I sallied forth on a mincemeat mission.

Which was surprisingly successful. While I won't go so far as to say it's a revelation (that's the sort of thing I reserve for discovering no-knead bread), it's not difficult. And it's delicious. And you can leave out all the bits you don't like, such as candied peel and weird fluorescent cherries, and put in more of what you do like, such as dates and apricots. I mean, you could even make a tropical version, if you were the sort of person who liked dried tropical fruits. You can make it boozy with brandy or rum, or keep it mellow with juice. It's easy, adaptable, and entirely worth doing.

And if you want to make mince pies with it, I shall add my favourite pastry recipe below (it's previously been in *Yule Be Sorry*).

Mincemeat:

- 175 g / 1 cup / 6 oz currants
- 175 g / 1 cup / 6 oz raisins
- 175 g / 1 cup / 6 oz chopped dates
- 175 g / 1 cup / 6 oz dried cranberries
- 100 g / just under ⅔ cup / 3 ½ oz chopped dried apricots
- 100 g / ½ cup / 3 ½ oz coconut oil
- 110 g / ½ cup / just under 4 oz soft light brown sugar
- 110 g / ½ cup / just under 4 oz soft dark brown sugar
- 50 g / ½ cup / ¾ oz flaked almonds
- 2 medium apples, peeled and grated
- zest and juice of one orange
- 1–2 tsp grated fresh ginger, to taste
- 1 tsp cinnamon
- a whole load of grated nutmeg

- ⅛ tsp ground cloves
- chopped fresh rosemary (optional)
- 240 mL / 1 cup alcohol or juice of choice (I actually used a ginger and lemongrass cordial, made up with water; it's an excellent non-alcoholic option)

Combine everything except the alcohol/juice in a large saucepan and heat gently. Once the coconut oil has melted, continue to simmer for about 10 minutes.

Remove from heat and stir in the alcohol or juice. Decant into sterilised jars and seal. If you've used alcohol, it'll keep for months. If not, you'll still get a good month out of it.

Go forth and make mince pies! Or just give away jars as gifts, and let people make their own. You've already done the hard bit.

Mince pies:

- 225 g / 1 cup / 8 oz cold butter, diced
- 350 g / just over 2 cups plain flour
- 100 g / ½ cup light brown sugar
- 280 g / a little more than 1 cup / 10 oz mincemeat
- 1 small egg
- Icing sugar to dust

Rub butter into flour until fully combined – you could do this in a food processor, but the less you work it, the more delicate the pastry will be, so by hand is gentler.

Mix in the sugar and a pinch of salt, then work lightly into a ball (don't add any liquid, even if it feels crumbly). The mix will be firm, and more like shortbread dough than pastry. You can use it immediately or chill for later.

Preheat oven to 200°C / just under 400°F. Using two mince pie tins (these are much shallower than muffin tins – about half the depth or even less. But I have used muffin tins before and just half-filled them, which worked okay, although getting them out was a bit tricky), press small balls of pastry (about a tablespoon) across the base and up the sides. Try to get the thickness as uniform as possible – the pastry is too soft to roll, so you'll need to get your hands in there. You should get about 18, with enough left over for the tops.

Spoon mincemeat into bases, then take slightly smaller scoops of pastry and pat them into lids in your hands. Top the pies with them and press edges together to seal. Alternatively, you can just dot scraps of pastry over the top of the pie rather than making a lid. These will spread to form a crumble-like top, which looks pretty and is lovely if you don't like too much pastry.

If you'd like to freeze your pies, this is the moment! Otherwise bake for about 20 minutes or until pastry is golden, then let rest in the tins for 5 minutes or so before lifting them gently out with a knife or fish slice. They are delicate, but *delectable.*

11
ELEVEN PIPERS PIPING

Alice rolled over to look at the window, the faintly darker smudge of the heavy curtains sealing out the night beyond, and wondered what had woken her. The house lay silent and empty, not even Thompson the cat prowling the darkness. He hadn't been around for at least two weeks, and she wondered where he'd got to. Not that she missed him, of course. And it wasn't as if he were *her* cat. She had merely become accustomed to the warm, relaxed weight of him curled next to her, or sprawled across the bottom of the bed, purring and shedding with equal enthusiasm.

She got up and took her dressing gown from behind the door, moving a little stiffly with the cold and the hour, then padded downstairs barefoot. She switched on the kitchen light, squinting against the brightness, and flicked the kettle on. There was no use trying to sleep once one started thinking about what cats did in their spare time.

The clock on the wall stood at quarter to four, and she sat down at the kitchen table while she waited for the kettle to boil. Her eyes were itchy, and her hip hurt from two days on her feet in the cold, and there was still another full day of market duty today. At least yesterday had been free of aggressive wreaths, angry turtles, and troublesome shelf elves. Mortimer had spent a lot of time at the back of the stall, glaring at the wreaths and getting through a staggering amount of mince pies, while Alice had glimpsed Amelia halfway up the Christmas tree, having a whispered argument with a dryad. There had also been rather a lot of very suspicious-looking dogs wandering around unattended that no one had paid much attention to.

Alice couldn't understand how anyone was taken in by the dog suits, with their oversized tails and smoke drifting from the nostrils, but people saw what they expected to see. Other than a few overexcited children who had higher expectations of reality than their parents, everyone apparently just saw some large dogs of uncertain parentage. Although that annoying reporter had been poking around again – she'd spotted him taking photos and chatting to some of the stallholders, all while studiously avoiding the W.I. stall. She didn't particularly trust *him* not to see dragons. After all, he'd already seem them twice, so it didn't seem too much of a stretch to imagine he might see them again, and this time Thompson wasn't around to convince him otherwise.

Alice surprised herself by wishing the cat were there, and got up to fill the teapot.

SHE WAS SITTING at the table, sipping her tea and flicking through the local magazine while she tried to find the energy to make some sticky buns with the leftover mincemeat, when she stopped suddenly. She looked at her bag, hanging on the hook by the door next to her hat and scarf.

"Oh dear," she said, and got up, taking the bag down to check it. It had been so *cold* the night before, and between the worry of sneaking dragons and muttering dryads and some suspicious splashing going on in the well on top of the concerns of the stall, it had all felt like a terrible rush at the end of the day. She hadn't even gone to the pub with everyone else for a drink, but had come straight back here and climbed into a hot bath. She'd brought the cash box home with her, of course, and it was in the back of the pantry, behind the big bags of flour, but ...

"Oh dear," she said again, and hurried upstairs to put some outdoor clothes on. It really had been *terribly* busy, and they'd sold such a lot that the notes wouldn't all fit in the cash box (and it looked awfully crass, all that money sticking out every time they served someone). She'd taken some out and bundled it tightly in a bag, and tucked the bag in among the spare cups for the mulled wine, where no one would see it. Not even her, it turned out. And it might be four in the morning, but she wasn't going to sit here making breakfast buns and worrying about it. Being tired and careless was one thing. Not fixing the problem as soon as she was aware of it was quite another.

THE STREETS WERE DESERTED, the houses dark other than the odd light on in a bathroom or kitchen, other sleepless souls drifting in the empty hours. The stars were out, and a heavy frost made the gardens appear wrought from shattered glass, the trees gilded in silver. Alice drove slowly toward the centre of town, the car a cocoon of warmth around her. There was no point rushing. If anyone had been raiding stalls in the night then she was too late already, and if not, there was plenty of time to retrieve the money before the day started and the W.I. realised she'd forgotten it. Not that it *really* mattered if they knew, but, well ... it did. It seemed like a terribly inefficient and forgetful thing to do. An *old* thing to do. And it was quite bad enough knowing that about herself. She didn't need anyone else realising it too.

The Christmas lights flushed the village square, lighting the ghost town of canvas and wooden stalls with a cheery glow, and the Christmas tree glittered under its load of frost and ribbons and baubles as Alice parked. She turned off the engine and sat there in the heavy silence for a moment, watching, but there was no movement in the stalls or the tree, or even in the streets leading off the square. Not that she could see, anyway. She adjusted her woolly hat over her ears and climbed out, taking her cane with her. It was the one with the silver dragon's head and the repaired split where she'd used it on some goblins. It would be handy both for any icy patches and if the market wasn't as empty as it looked. One could never be too careful.

The aisles between the stalls were empty, any rubbish already swept and gone, leaving the market fresh for the next day. The stalls themselves presented blank, featureless faces to her, and no noises drifted from inside any of them. Across the road, there was a light on in the back of the bakery, and the rich scent of baking bread hung heavy in the air, making Alice's stomach rumble. She looked at her watch. She still had time to make some buns, and, that decided, she hurried straight to the W.I. stall. It took only a moment to unhook the ties holding the canvas side down, and unzip it enough that she could slip inside. It was dark under the heavy white canvas, and she turned on the torch on her phone, examining the stall. Nothing was disturbed. Plates and napkins were stacked to one side, more napkins and cups to the other, where the urns would be. The few unsold baubles and biscuit jars were lined up on a table at the back, and everything still smelled faintly of spilled mulled wine.

Alice crouched down to hunt through the extra paper cups under the counter, having a moment of fright when she felt nothing but more cardboard tubes, then her hand closed on the bundle of notes on the second pass.

"There we go," she said, fishing it out. "How silly of me." She straightened up, tucked the money into her coat, and let herself back out of the tent, her mind already on the breakfast buns. If she got them started as soon as she got home, she'd have time to let them cool enough to put a little glaze on top. It'd be a lovely treat for everyone to start the day with.

She hooked the last tie into place, turned to start back to the car, and stopped. A reedy, mournful sound washed over the village square, a tune that tugged at the mind, both irritating and vaguely enticing, familiar and not. Alice listened for a moment, finding her foot wanting to tap out a tune she could have sworn she didn't know, then crept forward a couple of steps so she could peer down the lane of stalls. The music was no louder here – it seemed to be coming from everywhere and nowhere at once, like the annoying music in department stores. She hesitated, then gripped her cane a little more firmly and headed toward the centre of the village square, the piping tune surrounding her.

The old well with its bucketless winch crouched next to the makeshift stage in the shadow of the Christmas tree, and when Alice peered out from the shelter of the nearest stall she could see the wreaths and baubles smothering its waist-high stone wall. Perched both on top of the wall and on the neat slate roof were … creatures. She couldn't have said what they were, even with the ever-expanding collection of folklore titles in her little library. She had assumed from the start that most of what was in her books was a mix of conjecture and exaggeration, but she was starting to suspect that they were, in fact, out and out fabrication. Certainly their descriptions of dragons were rather slanderous, and as for the creatures in front of her – well, she had no idea what they might be. They were small and angular and barefoot, and they were playing pipes with their eyes closed and their large, leathery wings trembling with emotion. Or possibly cold, but it looked like emotion.

Which was an odd enough thing to encounter in the village square, even at this hour of the morning, but they weren't alone. Surrounding them, swaying gently to the tune, were the owners of the dodgy pub (him in fancy silk pyjamas and her in a Guinness T-shirt and bright red shorts), and the bookshop owner wearing very little, and half a dozen other people Alice didn't immediately recognise, all in their nightclothes. Their eyes were open, but they didn't seem to be seeing anything, and the ground around them was crowded with sparrows and pigeons, all bobbing their heads rhythmically.

Alice checked on the pipers. They were still playing, small feet beating time on the well, paying no attention to the sleeping crowd. Movement caught her eye, and she spotted the lady from the unpleasant tea shop stumbling into the square in a heavy metal band T-shirt. Her retriever padded after her, whining unhappily, but the teashop lady just swayed to a halt and started headbanging slowly, her outstretched arms catching the bookshop owner's hairnet and knocking it off. No one seemed to notice.

She couldn't leave them here. She didn't know what sort of spell the creatures were casting, but she didn't see any way this could end well. If nothing else, they were all going to get frostbite on their bare feet. And there was no one she could call at four in the morning who'd be any use whatsoever. She'd just have to see if she could wake them herself. She took a step forward, and someone hissed, "Wait!"

Alice jumped back, startled, and looked around. "Oh," she said. "It's you. Hello, Mr Giles."

"Ervin," the journalist said, and gave her that dimpled grin. His dark hair was trapped under a woolly hat and he was wearing a coat with far too many pockets to be practical. His legs stuck out under it, looking twice as skinny as normal. "You're not going out there, are you?"

"These people are halfway to hypothermia already, Mr Giles. They're evidently sleepwalking, and I can't just *leave* them." He hadn't said anything about the pipers, so she had no intention of drawing his attention to them.

"Sleepwalking, right." He nodded, watching two more people slouch into the square. One of them trod on a pigeon, who pecked the man's toes. He didn't react. "So our weird little winged music band there is nothing to do with it, then?"

Alice sighed. So much for that. Evidently the journalist was predisposed to seeing Folk, or Thompson's hypnosis trick hadn't taken as well as the cat had declared it would. "Well. We seem to be fine, so don't you think we should help them?"

"I'm more interested in why it's happening," Ervin said, snapping a couple of photos on his phone. "There's all sorts of weird things going on in this village. And you lot are *always* involved, along with our erstwhile DI Adams. She's not here, is she?" he added, craning his neck to look down the aisle.

"I'm afraid not, Mr Giles. And I don't know what you think is happening—"

"The thing is, I've been close before. I know I have. Yet I've got these blank spots in my memory now, and they're always around you and DI Adams. Any idea what that's about?"

Alice sighed. Journalists were always so *trying*. So sure of themselves, and unfortunately quite accurate at times. "Mr Giles—"

"Ervin."

"If you must. Those people are going to freeze. Look!" She pointed across the square, to where more sleepwalkers were shambling toward the pipers, all in bare feet or fluffy socks, and not a one in so much as a dressing gown, let alone a coat. One young man was only wearing some very small shorts indeed, and Alice averted her eyes after noting he either had a very physical job or spent far more time than was healthy at the gym.

Ervin folded his arms. "I'll help. But not until you tell me what's going on."

Alice shook her head. "Young man, you have no sense of responsibility."

"I think you – or your group – *did* something to me to make me forget. Forgive me for not rushing into this without some guarantee I'll remember it."

They glared at each other across the aisle as a few more people ambled past. The little square around the well and the tree was starting to get quite crowded now, the sparrows and pigeons protesting as more feet pushed through them, the sleepwalkers trying to get closer to the well and the pipers. Alice could *feel* the tune now, humming in her ears like a second pulse and reverberating in the canvas of the stall behind her. Under it whispered the steady scuff of bare feet, men and women drifting past her in various states of undress, trailing worried dogs and comforters and stuffed toys and—

"No children," Ervin said. "See that?"

Alice blinked at the crowd. She was more tired than she'd thought, not to notice that. "You're quite right," she said. "How odd."

The journalist looked from the crowd to her. "Sure," he said. "*That's* odd."

Alice reached out and snagged the pyjama sleeve of a short, rather rotund man with impressive eyebrows. "Mr Norton?" she said. He kept moving, and she tightened her grip. "*Mr Norton.* You have to wake up."

He whined, a petulant, wordless sound, and tried to pull away. The piping rose a notch, and someone ran into the back of him. They growled their irritation, and Mr Norton tried to pull away again.

"Wake up," Alice insisted, then yelped and released him as he lunged at her. She ducked away from his outstretched arms and into the growing crowd. Mr Norton kept trundling forward, straight into the side of the stall where she'd been standing, then tripped over one of the base blocks and tumbled to the ground.

Ervin grabbed Alice and pulled her against the stall on the other side of the aisle. "They're not going to wake up."

"There has to be a way," she said, although her heart was going too fast. "We can't just leave them."

"Sod that. There's too many. And I doubt anyone's going to be any happier than him if we try it."

They both watched Mr Norton, who seemed to have forgotten how to get up and was rolling around on the cobbles, whining as the piping rose louder.

"We need to try," Alice said, just as Mr Norton rolled into the aisle and two more sleepwalkers tripped over him, crashing to the ground like felled trees and entirely blocking the way. Behind them, the others started to growl and whine, trying to stumble over the roadblock without much success.

"Come on," Ervin said, and they inched their way toward the square with their backs to the canvas, keeping an eye on the bottleneck behind them. The piping was still rising, becoming a wail that made the hair on Alice's neck stand to attention, and she peered through the throng ahead of them, trying to spot a piper.

She did. He was standing at the edge of the square, child-sized among the adults, and was still playing, his eyes narrow and infuriated. Alice stopped where she was, and Ervin bumped into her. "Oh dear," she said.

Ervin followed her gaze, said something stronger, and tried to retreat, pulling her with him. But the way back was jammed by the pileup, which was getting worse by the moment. "Into the stall," he said, grabbing for the zipper. "Hurry!"

The piping changed note again, and the army of sleepers

lurched to look in their direction, even the pigeons turning. Another of the pipers had left the well and come to stand next to the first. She was wearing a pink T-shirt that said *Christmas Angel*, and her long ears trembled with fury.

"Wait," Alice said, as Ervin ducked into the stall. "They can't stop playing. See? If we can get the pipes off even one of them, the spell's going to break."

"Are you sure?" Ervin asked, as a sleeper lurched toward them. He shoved the man back clumsily.

"Fairly."

"Oh, *well*. In that case." But he snatched a jar of olives from inside the stall and hefted it at the pipers. The first one ducked, and Christmas Angel ignored it entirely as it sailed harmlessly past her, only to hit a sleepwalker in the shoulder and send them stumbling to their knees. "Oops."

"Wonderful," Alice said, and grabbed her cane in both hands, using it to push a sleeper back. She stepped into the gap he left and did the same again.

"Hang on!" Ervin shouted, stumbling after her with an armful of jars.

"Hurry up, then." She shoved the shirtless young man away, keeping her eyes on the pipers. They were only a few metres away now. Ervin flung a few more jars, all of which exploded on the cobbles, and she tutted. "Someone's going to step on that. Just help me, can't you?"

"I thought I was." But he joined her, pushing the sleepwalkers back. They didn't seem aggressive as such, it was just that there were so terribly many of them, all pushing forward in a horrible crush of flannel and old T-shirts, crowding in from all sides. Ervin put his shoulder to a rather large woman in an even larger floral nightshirt, and as he forced her out of the way the pipers were suddenly right there.

Alice stepped forward and swung the cane, the arc fast and

sharp, and as it whistled toward the pipers someone grabbed her, pulling her back and sending the swing wide. Christmas Angel winked at her and kept playing, and Alice twisted away from her attacker, raising the cane to find old Mrs Garvey, who fed the ducks and knitted sweaters for penguins, clinging to her with the determination of a terrier. Alice lowered the cane and tried to wriggle free. She could hardly hit Mrs Garvey. It'd be like hitting one of those penguins.

"Ervin!" she shouted. "I can't reach them!"

He shouted something she couldn't quite understand from the middle of a crush of bodies. The pipes were roaring now, a wild, insistent tone, and the vibrations were singing in her bones. She tried once more to push Mrs Garvey away, but all the strength seemed to have left her limbs, and she dropped the cane, covering her ears with both hands. The music rose and rose, drowning Ervin's shouts and the growls of the sleepers, eternal and unstoppable and covering the world.

Then a hard, familiar voice cut through it all, coming from somewhere around her knees. "I go away for *two weeks.*"

"Thompson?" Alice managed.

"I take a little R and R after what has been a seriously stressful year, thanks to you lot, and I come back to a cold, empty house, no food left out, and *faeries.* Gods-damned faeries. I mean, what could you do if I left you for a *month?*"

And then he was gone, and the music faltered. Alice felt it drop from her like a loss, lightening and horrifying her all at once, and she gasped, shoving Mrs Garvey back and snatching up her cane. She pushed past a couple of swaying sleepers and spotted the two pipers, one still playing desperately while Christmas Angel braced her feet against the cobbles, trying to pull her pipes back from Thompson. His ragged ears were back and he was still grumbling, if inaudibly.

More pipers – or faeries, if the cat was to be believed – dashed toward them from the well, and Alice rushed forward with the cane raised as one of them aimed a kick at Thompson, still piping. The faery's tune faltered as he squeaked and jumped back, and Alice dealt him a smart smack on the head that made him drop his pipes entirely. Ervin darted out of the crowd to grab them up, shoving them in a pocket as Alice aimed a blow at Christmas Angel. She shrieked and let go of the pipes, and Thompson promptly vanished, taking them with him. Christmas Angel leaped up with her sharp teeth bared, glaring at Alice, and Alice pointed the cane at her.

"Stop it," she said.

"Will not," Christmas Angel said, waving at the other pipers to keep playing, even though the tune was weakening. Thompson reappeared without the pipes, making Ervin yelp, and tackled the nearest faery, cutting the strength of the tune further as he took them to the ground. Ervin pulled his scarf off and used it to lasso another piper, sweeping her off her feet and grabbing her pipes before she could recover. He dropped her and moved on to the next, and she promptly scrambled straight up his back and bit his ear. He howled.

"This is unacceptable," Alice said.

"It's an *outrage*," Christmas Angel said. "Meddlesome bloody humans!"

Alice feinted at her with the cane as Thompson captured another set of pipes and disappeared with them, and another faery joined the first on Ervin's shoulders. He was still trying to pull the first off. The music had all but stopped, and the crowd were just standing in place, as if waiting for instructions.

"What on earth did you think you were going to do with them all?" Alice asked, as Christmas Angel snarled at her.

"March them off the nearest cliff, probably," Christmas Angel said, and grinned. Alice caught the sudden look the faery flicked over her shoulder, and she ducked, bringing the cane up to meet another piper and sending him spinning to the ground. He squawked, and Ervin ripped his pipes away before he could recover, then looked up just in time to see yet another faery rushing him. He squawked and punched her, more luckily than efficiently.

"Sorry!" he shouted, and went back to trying to dislodge the faeries on his back. There were three of them now, and he'd lost his hat.

"You may as well give up," Alice said to Christmas Angel. The last of the piping was fading away, the few faeries who'd kept hold of their instruments looking around warily. Thompson kept appearing out of nothing and attacking them, and Alice had the feeling he was enjoying himself far more than he should be. "Even if we weren't here, you don't have enough pipes now, do you?"

Christmas Angel glared at her, then looked at the sleepers in the square. Quite a few of them had laid down on the cobbles and were snoring contentedly. She sighed. "Pack it up," she said, twirling a taloned finger in the air. Ervin yelped as one of the faeries gave him a parting nip on the ear before jumping clear. Christmas Angel looked back at Alice. "Don't think I'm forgetting this, woman."

"I should hope not," Alice said. "Remembering should stop you doing it again." Her hip was hurting, but she stood perfectly straight, the tip of the cane on the ground in front of her and both hands folded over the head. "Now send all these people home and make sure they don't remember anything."

"No," the faery said.

"Yes," Thompson said, materialising next to Alice. "There are *treaties,* you buck-toothed, child-stealing green-skinned potato. What, you thought you could just steal a whole *town* and no one would notice? Enslave the adults and turn the kids? Those days are *done.*"

"Doesn't look like the rules much apply here," the faery said.

"Not with dragons all over the place like a nasty rash. Why shouldn't we get in on it too?"

"Because I won't have it," the cat said.

"You going to bring the wrath of the Watch down on me?" Christmas Angel asked, and grinned, showing those sharp grey teeth again. "Bet they'd have *lots* to say about dragon tea parties."

Thompson growled, and Alice said, "The Watch is one thing. But if you try *anything* like this again, it'll be the W.I. you have to deal with. And I do *not* recommend that."

The faery looked at her for a long, stretched moment, then hissed softly and turned away. "Mel, Georgia – play these meat-bag humans home." She clicked her fingers at Ervin, who blinked at her. "Pipes. I need some pipes. Whatever that flea-ridden cat hasn't dropped in the bloody Inbetween."

Ervin looked at Alice, who looked at Thompson. He nodded, she nodded, and Ervin gave the pipes cautiously back to the faeries and fumbled for his phone.

"No," Alice said, as the piping started up again, a gentle, soporific melody.

"Right," he replied, and put his hands in his pockets while they watched the townspeople slowly drifting back to empty beds with dirty feet they'd puzzle over in the morning.

Finally the square was empty except for the shuffling birds and the faeries. Christmas Angel looked at Thompson, then Alice. "Done," she said.

"Off you go, then," Thompson said. "Go dream about being as cutesy as humans think you are."

"I'll do it again in a heartbeat," she said, as the faeries unfolded leathery, strangely-jointed wings and took to the skies in a hum of wingbeats.

"Try it," Alice suggested, and smiled as the faery made a face at her. Then they were gone.

"Can't leave you alone for a moment, can I?" Thompson asked Alice.

"I don't see how you can blame any of this on me," she said. "One does not anticipate faery people-trafficking rings."

"Still," the cat said, and looked at Ervin. "As for you—"

"No!" he yelped, ducking behind Alice. "You stay away! It was you! You did something to me! *Twice!*"

"That sounds way worse than it is," Thompson said. "It's just a bit of memory adjustment."

"No! I just about fainted when I saw my mum's cat last week! I'm *traumatised!*"

"Look, just settle down a moment, and it'll all be done and you won't even remember—"

"I won't! Get away from me!"

"Thompson, stop it," Alice said, shaking Ervin off. He was clinging to her arm like a panicked swimmer. "He's evidently not going to keep forgetting, so I think it's best to explain the situation."

"He's a *journalist*," the cat said, making the word sound like a hairball. "That's dangerous."

"I rather think you poking around in his brain all the time is dangerous too."

"It'll only improve a journalist."

"Sod off," Ervin said, straightening his jacket. "I'm not being insulted by a *cat.*"

"You may have to get used to it," Alice said, taking her keys from her coat. "Come along, you two. We'll have a cup of tea and a chat."

"What sort of chat?" Ervin asked. "You can't buy me off, you know."

"Will there be salmon?" Thompson asked.

"There's tuna."

"It's *Christmas*. And I just saved you from a mob of faeries. What sort of host are you?"

"A tired one," Alice said, and led the way to her car with the cat and the journalist trailing behind. And she thought that might be at least a little bit of a lie, because her heart was alive with strange, wild magic, and she could feel the day creeping toward them, full of hope and promise and impossible things.

And also mincemeat buns, if she got started soon enough.

MINCEMEAT STICKY BUNS

Confession time. The only cinnamon rolls I've ever made are those ones that you buy in the fridge section, which come in a cardboard tube. They give a most satisfying *pop* as you open them, and you just wedge the buns in a pan and bung them in the oven. They even have a little pot of icing to smother them with before serving.

I've not actually had them since I worked in the Caribbean, so I'm not sure how widespread these buns are – they were an American product. They constituted my one cheat breakfast bread of the week when I was cooking, and I loved them. *Everyone* loved them.

Second confession: I always saved them for the last day, by which point the guests had seen me making everything from scratch all week. I'm fairly sure only a handful of people ever realised that their delicious last-day breakfast was partly catered by buns-in-a-tube.

I've never felt any real *need* to recreate cinnamon rolls until recently. I think it coincided with my discovery that I could make bread without kneading, including cinnamon-y breads. And then somewhere I saw a mincemeat sticky bun, and, *well.* We just made all that lovely mincemeat. We can't eat it *all* in mince pies, can we?

Besides, a bread roll stuffed with mincemeat is somehow more acceptable for breakfast than a pastry shell stuffed with mincemeat. I'm not *entirely* clear on why, but these are the rules.

For the dough:

- 250 mL / 1 cup milk
- 50 g / 3 ½ Tbsp / 1 ¾ oz butter
- 50 g / 3 ½ packed Tbsp / 1 ¾ oz soft brown sugar
- 7 g / 2 tsp active dry yeast
- 450 g / 3 ½ cups bread flour
- 1 ½ tsp cinnamon
- 1 tsp salt
- ½ tsp mixed spice
- 1 large egg, beaten

For the filling:

- 50 g / 3 ½ Tbsp / 1 ¾ oz butter
- 25 g / 1 ¾ packed Tbsp / just under 1 oz soft brown sugar
- 300 g / 1 ⅓ cups / 10 ½ oz mincemeat
- 100 g / ⅓ cup nuts or extra dried fruit (optional, depending on how loaded you want them)

Heat the milk over a low heat until it steams, then remove from the heat and stir in the butter and a spoonful of the sugar. Cool until lukewarm, then whisk in the yeast and set aside until it's nice and foamy.

Mix all the dry ingredients together, then add the yeast mix and the egg. Mix well, then knead for 5–10 minutes, until you can stretch a small piece of the dough thin without it tearing (the "windowpane" test). You could also throw it in a standing mixer with a dough hook for around 5 minutes.

Cover and allow to rise in a warm place until doubled in size, which'll take 1–2 hours, depending on how warm it is where you are. Alternatively, pop it in the fridge and come back the next morning.

Give the dough another quick knead (if it was in the fridge you'll need to bring it to room temperature first), then roll it out to roughly 45 x 40 cm / 16 x 18 inches.

Melt the butter for the filling and brush it generously over the dough. Sprinkle with the sugar, keeping a little back, then spread your mincemeat and extras evenly over the top.

Starting from the long side, roll up tightly. Cut off the ends to tidy it up, then slice into 8. Pop in a greased pan or tray with about 1 cm between them, cover and allow to double again. This time should be quicker – half an hour to an hour. When they're almost ready, preheat the oven to 190°C / 350°F.

Sprinkle with the remaining sugar and bake for about 20–25 minutes, or until nicely browned on top. Either glaze immediately with some melted apricot jam, or allow to cool and add icing. Eat that day, or freeze for future festive breakfasts.

12
TWELVE DRUMMERS DRUMMING

With a certain grim measure of self-discipline, DI Adams resisted the urge to either put her head in her hands or scream, and instead said in a calm voice, "So you've been attacked by rogue elf-on-the-shelfs ... elves-on-the-shelves—"

"Just one elf," Gert said. "Eight milkmaids, though."

"Right. Rogue milkmaids—"

"China ones, I mean. Not real milkmaids."

"Do they still have milkmaids?" Teresa asked. "That seems a bit condescending. Milk*maids.*"

"And what if one were male?" Rose asked. "Or undefined? Shouldn't it be milk-person?"

"Milk-technician," Priya suggested.

"That sounds like a kitchen gadget," Pearl said. "You know, for frothy coffees."

There was a murmur of agreement and Adams leaned back in one of the high-backed kitchen chairs that had been brought into the living room for extra seating. The screaming option was holding a certain appeal. The high ceilings and big windows of

Alice's front room should have kept it cool, but although the room was a decent size, it wasn't designed to hold the ten members of the Toot Hansell Women's Institute, herself, Collins, and bloody Ervin, the journalist. Plus Dandy, who was lying next to Pearl's ancient Labrador, snuffling her ear while she pointedly ignored him. There was also a steady yapping coming from the kitchen, where Jasmine's Pomeranian was shut in, and the whole place just felt far too crowded and overwhelming for barely being eight in the morning.

She took a deep breath and spoke over the discussion, which was still milk-centred. *"As I was saying,"* she said, "You then had a Christmas garland attack—"

"Apparently that was dryads," Miriam said. She was very pink and wearing a large blue skirt with Christmas puddings appliquéd to the hem, and she kept peering out the windows. DI Adams supposed she was looking for dragons, which was all they needed – the journalist had already seen more than enough of Toot Hansell's secrets.

"Great," she said. "So, rogue elves – sorry, one elf and eight milkmaids – dryads setting wreaths on you, then the bloody pied pipers of Toot Hansell calling half the village out of their beds, and you only call us *now?*"

"Faeries," Thompson said. He was perched on the arm of Alice's sofa, his kinked tail curled over his toes and his tatty ears up. "Not pipers. Evil little snot-faced faeries. And make sure you pronounce that with an A-E. They can tell if you don't."

"Faeries," DI Adams said.

"Faeries," Thompson insisted.

"I *said*— never mind. My point is, all I knew about were geese and bloody swans. A heads-up *before* the market was under attack might've been nice."

"To be fair, Detective," Alice said, "None of it *really* seemed to be the jurisdiction of the police until the attempted abductions."

"Geese," DI Adams said. "You called us for the *geese.*"

"That was me," Miriam said. "I may have overreacted a smidge."

"You didn't," DI Adams said. "I think the rest of you are all *under*-reacting."

"Come on, Adams," Collins said, around a large bite of bacon butty. The journalist was sitting cross-legged on the floor next to him, working on his own sandwich and being uncharacteristically quiet. DI Adams looked at the sticky mincemeat bun on her own plate and sighed. She seemed to have lost her appetite.

"Come on *what*? How are we meant to help when no one tells us anything?"

"It's Christmas," Collins pointed out, wiping brown sauce from the corner of his mouth. "The ladies know we're busy, and I imagine everyone thought the dra—"

He was drowned out by the clamour of the Women's Institute suggesting more tea, or possibly another sticky bun, and look – was that the time? They needed to get to the market. The stall wasn't going to set itself up. Collins looked at the journalist and took an enormous bite of his sandwich, apparently deciding he was better off with his mouth full. DI Adams massaged the sides of her head, where the hair felt pulled too tight. It had been a rush to get ready that morning.

"Okay, okay," she said over everyone. "You're right, I'm sorry, and let's take it from there. What's happening today?"

"It's the final day of the market," Alice said. "It's Christmas Eve tomorrow, so I imagine this could all be over in a couple of days. Don't you think so, Thompson?"

The cat shrugged. "It's not an exact science, kids. It's Saturnalia today, so it could all be over tonight, even. Who knows?"

A murmur of muted relief greeted that, then Miriam said, "Unless it's about Yule. Then it won't be done until the first of January."

"But if it was because of Yule, didn't all this start too early?" Rose asked.

"Do we even know when it really started?" Carlotta asked. "What was the first thing?"

No one had an answer to that, and after a moment they all looked at Thompson. He narrowed his eyes. "Humans. You're always looking for patterns and explanations and trying to make things *fit*. Folk have their own reasons. Or they don't. Who knows, really?"

There was silence for a moment, then DI Adams said, "You are just so helpful. Even better than Dandy." Dandy lifted his head off his paws and looked at her.

Thompson spat. "That monster's a menace."

DI Adams felt the hard, healing scabs on her hands rasp against her mug and nodded. "Undoubtedly. However, he doesn't talk as much rubbish as some people I could mention."

"Um. Can I just ask what sort of monster a Dandy is?" Ervin asked, raising one hand a little as if trying to get attention in class. "I'm starting to lose track."

DI Adams frowned at him. She didn't like him being here. He'd been banned from taking notes or touching his phone, and this was the first thing he'd said since she and Collins had arrived, but his quick dark eyes missed nothing. She'd half hoped he'd be too shocked by the faery encounter to believe what was happening, but he seemed irritatingly comfortable with the conversation. He also looked more awake than she felt, which was even more irritating.

"He's just a dandy," she said.

"He's an invisible dog," Collins said helpfully. "Although I did see him once, when he was really angry."

"He's the worst," Thompson said.

Dandy growled, very softly, and Pearl's Labrador *whuff*ed her disapproval.

Ervin brushed crumbs from his hands, careful to catch them on his plate. His hair was dishevelled, curling around his ears and the base of his neck, and he had scratches on his forearms where his sleeves were pushed up. "Right. So, what happens now? How do we stop whatever's coming today? Because something else is going to happen, isn't it?"

'No," DI Adams and Collins said together.

"Well, it *sounds* like something's going to happen."

"No as in, no, *we're* not doing anything," DI Adams said. *"We,"* and she pointed at Collins and herself, "might be, but you're heading back to Leeds to cover the scandal of overpriced beer at the Christmas market there."

"Unfair," Ervin said, frowning at her.

"Well, you can't report this," Miriam said, her eyes wide. "You *can't!* It'll put the dra—"

A surge of chatter rose over her, and Gert pulled herself out of the sofa, stooping to take Ervin's plate. "Off you go, then," she told him.

"I never once said I was going to report *any* of this," he protested. "I want to help!"

"And we'd trust you?" Rose demanded. "Damn hacks and their stories."

"That's even more unfair," Ervin said, and looked around. "Alice?"

"Ms Martin," Priya said, glowering at him in a surprisingly effective manner, considering she and Jasmine were wedged onto a pouffe together, neither of them looking very secure.

"Alice is fine," Alice said. "He did very well this morning. He may be useful."

Ervin looked like he didn't know whether to be offended or complimented, and DI Adams raised her eyebrows at Alice. The older woman gave something that was halfway between a shrug and a nod. Well. It was better than the journalist poking around on his own, she supposed. This way at least they could keep an eye on him.

"So what now?" Teresa asked, looking at her watch. "We really do need to be getting to the market to set up."

"Why don't you carry on?" Alice suggested. "Ervin can help, and Miriam and I will catch up with you shortly."

"I'd rather catch up later, too," Ervin said, but Rosemary and Carlotta were already helping him to his feet.

Carlotta squeezed one of his arms as they led him to the door. "Nice strong young man like you," she said. "You'll have all the mulled wine moved in a jiffy."

"It's that or doing dishes here," Rosemary agreed. "No one would prefer *that*."

"Well," Ervin tried, as he was propelled inexorably down the hall. "I don't *mind* dishes. And someone's got to do them, right?"

"I hope you're not the sort of boy who doesn't help his elders," Carlotta said. "You're not, are you?"

"No," Ervin said, looking alarmed, and DI Adams leaned out of the living room door to watch Gert piling crates of mince pies in his arms. "Um ..." He looked around and caught her eye, and she grinned, then ducked back into the living room. Collins and Miriam were collecting plates as the rest of the W.I. piled out, donning scarves and hats and gloves and an astonishing array of coats, and Alice was still sitting in her armchair, rubbing her forehead.

"Are you alright?" DI Adams asked her.

"I will be," Alice said. "Let's just hope we can get through this without him stumbling on dragons, shall we?"

"Sure," Thompson said from under the coffee table, where he was chewing on some bacon. "Because faeries are so much easier to explain."

❄

THE DAY FELT FRAUGHT. It didn't help that both Collins and DI Adams kept getting calls from the station in Skipton, and explaining that they were in Toot Hansell chasing leads somehow didn't sit that well with the DCI.

"But *what* leads?" she demanded of DI Adams. "What *case?*"

"It's ... ah, it's connected to the break-in."

"*Which* break-in, Adams? We do have more than one a year up here, you know, even if the crime rate's not what you're used to."

"Um. The ... the one in Helwith Bridge. With the presents."

"Huh. Connected, is it?"

"We think so, yes."

"And it takes both of you to investigate the theft of some presents, does it?"

DI Adams took a breath. "Yes. I mean, to get the leads run down quicker, you know."

"And so I should find the case report around here somewhere, should I? Even though I've heard *nothing* about any incident in Toot Hansell."

DI Adams supposed that was a good thing. At least no one other than Alice and the journalist had noticed the sleepwalkers last night. "It's just a possible connection we're running down."

There was a long pause, and she heard the DCI take a sip of coffee. "Alright," the DCI said finally. "If only because Collins is out there with you, and he wouldn't be off on a wild goose chase. Although he's not making much more sense than you are."

DI Adams, thinking that they had, in fact, been on a wild goose chase a couple of days ago, said, "We were out pretty early."

The DCI *hmph*ed and said, "I know Toot Hansell gets weird. Just remember that it's Christmas, and *everywhere's* weird."

The phone went dead, and DI Adams pocketed it with a sigh, rubbing her eyes. It was after lunch, and the day felt both stretched and too busy. Dragons in dubious disguises slipped among the stalls, heads low and strangely cautious, and creatures watched them from the trees. She supposed they must be the dryads. They looked put out, muttering to each other, and sometimes she caught movement on the roofs of the buildings that surrounded the square, although nothing was there when she looked again. There was also a surprising amount of what looked like garden gnomes camped out in clusters around the tables at the beer tent and the Viking bar, and you'd almost think they *were* garden gnomes, except that they changed position when you weren't looking. That, and they were looking distinctly less cute and more leering as the day went on.

She spotted Collins waving a bap at the cat, who was cleaning a paw, and wandered over to join them, tucking her hands into her pockets as she went.

"What're you doing?" she asked.

"Bigmouth here stole my sausage sandwich," Collins said.

"Didn't," the cat said. "I just took the sausage."

"Which is kind of the whole point of a sausage sandwich."

"Would you stop arguing with the cat?" DI Adams asked. "At least try and look like a regular, official sort of detective hanging around a village market for no reason."

"It's for your own good, anyway," Thompson said. "Bad for your cholesterol, all that bacon and sausage."

"He's got a point," DI Adams said, and ambled back to lean against the car, watching the shoppers threading their way between the stalls. Everything felt a little off, the laughter too shrill, the voices too bright. Everyone felt right on the verge of panic.

"I won't be lectured by a cat," Collins said, following her. "And it's the principle of the thing, really."

"Sure it is," she said. "You seen anything besides sausage sandwiches?"

"So much," he said. "But nothing threatening, exactly."

"Same."

They fell silent as they watched a moth-eaten Newfoundland with rather short legs and a lumpy back march up to them, accompanied by the cat. No one paid any attention to it except one small girl who waved a plastic sword excitedly and had to be dragged off by her parents.

"Detective inspectors!" the Newfoundland said. "It's me, Beaufort."

"You don't say," Collins said.

"Hello, Beaufort," DI Adams said.

"These disguises really do come in so handy," the High Lord said. "Most effective!"

The inspectors made non-committal noises, and Thompson snorted. "So, have you seen anything, oh Master of Disguise?"

Beaufort tried for a disapproving look, but it was a little lost though the eye holes, which weren't quite aligned properly. "Nothing yet. That journalist keeps following Mortimer around, though. The poor lad's beside himself and has gone to hide in the W.I. stall before he loses any more scales."

"The journalist's a bit of a problem," Collins said.

"He wouldn't be, if Alice'd just let me wipe his mind again," Thompson complained. "I mean, there's only a 50/50 chance it'll break him."

"Best leave it," DI Adams said. "A whole journalist's bad enough. I don't like the sound of a broken one."

"Very wise," Beaufort said. "Right. I shall head back and check on Mortimer and the ladies. One can't be too careful." He lumbered off, tail dragging through the icy puddles and looking increasingly threadbare.

"Check out the mince pies, more like," Thompson said, jumping onto the bonnet of the car and up to the roof, where he settled down with his feet tucked under him.

"Now *that's* wise," Collins said, and they watched the crowds ebb and flow through the stalls as the afternoon crept on into the early dark of the Saturnalia night.

Or Christmas Eve Eve.

Or the third day of Yule.

Or all of the above, or none, depending on your beliefs.

THERE WAS A BRIEF, yet entirely wonderful moment, when the sky darkened above the stalls and the lights were soft and warm, and the slightly panicked energy of the crowd had been mellowed by the mulled wine and hot chocolate, when DI Adams thought they were going to be alright. That maybe they had got things wrong, and maybe the faery pipers of the night before had been the end of it. Whatever *it* had been. She was even considering Gert's offer of a large glug of whisky in her coffee when Beaufort went thundering past the stall, huffing steam, his Newfoundland costume melting off his shoulder.

"Oh no," Miriam said, which seemed rather an understatement. Mortimer sprinted after the High Lord, wings straining at the seams of his disguise, and somewhere toward the centre of the market a scream went up.

DI Adams slammed her mug down, slopping coffee over her hand and the counter, and sprinted after the dragons, yelling for Collins as she went. She caught a flash of movement to the side of the stall, and Dandy joined her, running fast and silent with his grey hair flying back from his red eyes. Someone else was shouting, and ahead of them the screaming rose to a chorus.

She burst from the aisle of stalls into the central area of the market, the tree towering over the well at its cobbled heart. There were children everywhere, packed shoulder to shoulder, clutching hot chocolates and doughnuts and each other's hands, all huge grins and runny noses. Their eyes were fixed on a huge chair set on the stage, and the rotund figure rubbing his hands together eagerly. Little shrieks of excitement spread through the crowd like shockwaves.

"Ho, ho, ho," the figure said, and his belly actually did jiggle like jelly, which DI Adams blinked at. "Shall we see what's in the sack, little humans?" He sat down on the chair and beckoned a small girl forward from the crowd. She crept forward with her eyes wide, and cameras flashed around the square. There was a general *aww* from the adults as two elves (who had to be kids as well, right? To be that size?) helped her onto the stage.

"Beaufort!" Mortimer hissed, pulling DI Adams' attention off Santa. The young dragon was trying to block the High Lord's way. "No! You can't just run out there!"

"I'm not going to just stand here and *watch!*" Beaufort snapped. No one was paying them any attention. The adults were fixated on the children, and the children only had eyes for the big man in his red suit. The little girl was climbing onto his knee, her gloved hands tiny on his chest as she whispered in his ear.

"Beaufort, it's just Santa," DI Adams said. "It's okay."

"It's *not*," he insisted.

"Well, I mean, no, it's not *really* Santa. It's a man in a suit. I'm sure they do it every year."

"We do," Alice said, joining them. Her nose was pink with the cold. "It's a bit of a village tradition. The W.I. organises all the presents."

"See?" Mortimer said to the High Lord. "It's fine. Really."

"It's not," Beaufort said. "Something's off."

"A *pony?*" Santa shouted from the stage, and gave a thundering laugh. "How *original!* How *different!* Your parents must be *so proud!*"

A titter of uncertain laughter went up from the adults, and the kids looked at each other. The little girl stared up at Santa and said, "Well? Can I have one?"

"Well *of course*," Santa said, looming over her. He seemed taller, and the girl had to crane her neck to see his face. "Because I could *really* fit one of those in my sack, couldn't I?"

She frowned. "Well, it's a magic sack, isn't it?"

"More than you know," Santa said, and grinned, his mouth wide and wet in his beard. "But where would you keep it? How would you pay for it? You don't think of these things, do you, small creature? Behold, the future of humanity!" He bellowed laughter, and DI Adams was quite sure no one's belly should jiggle like that. "You lucky things!"

A couple of people laughed, but most of the adults were looking around as if they wanted someone else to say something, and a few of the smaller children were crying. The little girl glared up at Santa and shouted, "You're a *horrible* Santa! I hate you!"

"Oh, boohoo," Santa said, and grabbed her arm as she started to scramble off his lap.

"That's not our Santa," Alice said.

"I'd rather come to that conclusion," DI Adams said, and started pushing through the crowd.

Santa stood, lifting the girl by her arm. She screamed and booted him in the belly, which gave DI Adams quite a lot of hope for the future of humanity.

"Police!" she yelled. "Let me through! *Police!*" The crowd was packed so tightly it was hard to move, adults struggling to make way for her and kids staring up at her with astonished faces. She hoped no one was going to be too traumatised by seeing Santa arrested.

"Beaufort!" Alice shouted behind her. "*Do not* bite Santa!"

DI Adams had time to think that really might be more traumatising than seeing him arrested, as she scooped a small boy out of her path and shoved him at the nearest adult. "Clear the area!"

"Santa!" Collins shouted from the other side of the square. "Put that girl down *now!*"

"Sod off!" Santa yelled back. He was trying to stuff the girl in the sack, but she was wriggling so wildly he couldn't get his aim right. Two of the elves – who looked toothy and scrawny and not *at all* like the children DI Adams had assumed they were – were trying to get hold of the girl, but she'd already bitten one of them and the other looked a bit reluctant. The rest of the elves had dived into the crowd, and there were tug of wars happening as children tried to pull each other to safety, and the elves tried to pull them to the stage, and the adults couldn't seem to decide if this was all part of the show or not. One woman was shouting rather piercingly that she wished to speak to the manager, and a man was insisting he was going to write to the paper.

"North Yorkshire Police!" DI Adams bellowed, pulling an elf off a shrieking boy. *"Clear the—* Oh, sod it. *Beaufort, bite that bloody Santa!"*

But it wasn't Beaufort who came whooping through the crowd, swinging a small Christmas tree around his head and scattering baubles everywhere. It was the journalist, and he bounced onto the stage and aimed the tree at Santa's head like a novice cricketer hacking for a ball.

Santa roared and dropped the girl, batting the tree away. Ervin snagged her as she fell and shoved her behind him, and the jolly fat man grabbed him in two enormous white-gloved hands and lifted him effortlessly off the ground. Ervin screeched as he was tipped upside down and aimed at the sack, and DI Adams pulled the girl off the stage and pushed her toward Collins.

"North Yorkshire Police!" she shouted again, scrambling onto the stage. "Put him *down!*"

Santa stared at her, and she had a brief moment to wonder what had happened to her plans for a career of thwarting actual criminals, then he burst out laughing. "In the sack! In the sack with the North Yorkshire Police!"

So she punched him in the belly, which really did feel like punching a bowl of hot, claggy jelly, and which worked in that he dropped Ervin and grabbed her instead. He was far taller than he should be. "You're going on the naughty list," he said.

"I'm too old to be on the list," she said, glancing behind her. The square was in chaos, but there was sense to it. The dragons were surging out of hiding, snapping at elves, raising their wings to protect the fleeing children (well, most of them were fleeing. Three small girls were pummelling an elf with decorative candy canes, and a girl and a boy in matching hats were chasing another elf grimly across the square, waving sticks of nougat at him). Collins was still shouting somewhere, and she could hear Alice's voice raised over the commotion, ordering everyone out.

"No one's ever too old for *my* list," Santa said, and grinned at her. His teeth were long and terrible, and she was having to crane to look up at him, just as the little girl had. "And if you're naughty, it's into the sack with you!"

"I wish you'd stop saying naughty," she said, then yelped as he hefted her into the air, upending her and plunging her toward the sack, which yawned like some tear in reality itself, vast and bottomless and starving. She grabbed the edge of it, trying to brace herself against it, but it just collapsed in her grip, a cold wind wafting toward her that ate at her bones.

"A little help!" she yelled. "Dandy! *Dandy!*" She managed to push off the ground and swing toward Santa, flailing wildly, and her fingers snagged his beard. She tore at it and he roared, an echoing, ancient sound, then shoved her toward the maw of the sack again. She clung to his beard, twisting her fingers in it, and just as she thought he was going to pull her loose a Christmas pudding flew out of the night and splatted into his face, covering her with brandy-drenched fruit.

Santa spluttered, taking a step back, and a second pudding followed the first.

"Hey!" he roared, his grip on her legs loosening. "That's no way to treat Santa!"

DI Adams took up her weight on his beard and kicked, hard as she could. His grip had eased just enough that one leg jerked free, then the other, and she flopped to the floor, managing to get one foot to either side of the sack.

She looked up in time to see Dandy leap out of the crowd, lips pulled back from his teeth and red eyes bright, and flung herself sideways. He hit Santa in the belly, sending him staggering into the chair with an *oof*, and DI Adams rolled away from them. Ervin grabbed her arm, pulling her off the stage, and another Christmas pudding sailed past, followed by a large lump of fruitcake.

"What do we do?" Ervin asked, his eyes wide. "What now?"

DI Adams looked around. Dandy was still dancing around Santa, who had grabbed the sack and was trying to trap him in it, and at the edge of the square Teresa was throwing festive missiles with her eyes narrowed, Pearl and Priya keeping her stocked. Collins was tussling with a dryad at the foot of the Christmas tree while Amelia shouted that she was going to burn the whole place down and Gilbert shouted back that pacifism was a healthy choice. The rest of the dragons were facing down the elves, and otherwise the square was empty.

"Adams?" Ervin asked, and she looked at him, then at three elves edging around the stage. Their eyes glittered in the mellow lighting, and their outfits were looking distinctly tatty.

"He'll devour you all," one of them said, sounding rather pleased with the notion. "We're taking back Christmas, we are."

"You're a rubbish elf," DI Adams said.

"I'm a *faery*," the elf snarled. "And we're going to show you how the year really ends."

"That sounds bad," Ervin said, and Santa leaped from the stage with a wordless roar. The ground shook when he landed, his vast belly shaking, and he towered over the stalls, the red of his suit so deep it hurt the eyes.

"In the sack! In the sack with everyone!"

"Definitely bad," DI Adams said, and jumped as a wet nose touched her hand. She looked down at Dandy, and he nudged her again. She felt wet metal, and cupped her palm. He dropped the gold rings into it. She looked at them, then at Santa, still roaring and belly-laughing. The dragons were circling, trying to keep the faeries at bay, and a steady hail of Christmas treats was still raining over the square. Thompson was having a screaming match with one of the faeries. "What do I do with these?"

Dandy just waited, and she squeezed the rings, as if that would tell her what to do.

"I will destroy you!" Thompson screeched.

"Go call your precious Watch, then," the faery bawled back. "We've got *him!*" She waved at Santa, who made a grab for Lord Margery and got burned knuckles for his troubles. He wailed and stuck his fingers in his mouth.

Dandy nudged her again.

"What? What do I do—" She opened her hand, and stopped. The gold glittered, the heavy rings far bigger than the delicate circlets she'd tucked into her drawer days ago. These were the size … well, the size of handcuffs. And she knew handcuffs.

DI Adams took a step forward as Santa tried to shake off the combined assault of two slightly chubby dragons, one of whom was wearing a ski hat, and shouted, *"Police.* You're under arrest, Santa."

There was a strange, empty pause, while everyone stared at her, then the faeries burst out laughing and Santa did his wobbly belly thing again and reached for her with one huge fist.

And she threw the rings.

They flew in a perfect, curving arc, hitting the red expanse of his chest, and for one horrifying moment she thought they were going to just fall harmlessly to the floor. Then there was a *snap*, and the rings jolted away from each other, latching onto Santa's wrists and ankles, the fifth circling his neck. He yelped, tried to take a step, and staggered against some unseen restriction. He swayed, towering above the market square like a tree on the verge of toppling.

"Oh, bollocks," DI Adams said. *"Run!"*

There was a lot of confusion after that. Santa came crashing to the ground with a roar of despairing rage, the impact raising drifts of dropped cups and napkins, and Walter, who'd arrived slightly late, bit the first faery he saw, which set the rest of the faeries off. Beaufort was yelling for the Cloverlies to keep calm and take the high road, right up until a faery stabbed his tail with a fork, and he belched flame that set the bottom branches of the Christmas tree on fire and sent the dryads running out into the fray. Collins dived into the drinks tent and came out with a hose, which he tried to aim at the tree, but it only spluttered and spat uselessly, so he abandoned it and took his jacket off, thrashing the flames with it. Alice shouted for buckets as she ran to join him with an abandoned pint of beer in each hand, and Ervin was on the stage, peering into the sack.

DI Adams snatched it off him. "Stop that."

"He was trying to put us in it."

"I know that."

"Was that really Santa?"

"Of some description."

He shuddered, rather theatrically. "That'll give you nightmares."

She scowled at Dandy, who was tugging on the sack. "What?"

He kept tugging, so she followed him, and he led her off the stage and over to Santa, who glared up at her.

"This is so unfair," he said. "I thought the leprechauns took these damn rings ages ago."

"Huh," she said, and looked at Dandy. "Maybe they did."

"I suppose you're going to put me back in the bloody sack, too."

"Am I? I mean, I am," she added, as Dandy tugged the sack again. She scratched her forearm. Santa seemed a little smaller than he had, but she still couldn't exactly lift him in. She crouched down, though, and stretched the mouth of the sack over his big black boots, trying to ignore the draft of chill air that whispered out and raised the hair on her arms.

"This was *my* holiday," Santa said. "People had some respect. If they didn't leave decent gifts they knew they'd be on the naughty list, and I'd take their children away in my sack."

"Charming," DI Adams said, watching the sack. It was inching its way up Santa's legs, and he'd shrunk almost to the height of a man.

"Proper holiday, that was."

"I imagine," she said, as the sack swallowed his hips. He was shorter than her, now.

"You can't kill me, you know. I'll come back."

"I'll be here," she said, and smiled as the sack swallowed him.

"So THAT'S IT?" DI Adams asked. They were crowded around the counter of the W.I. stall, and the market was well and truly over. She and Collins had spent the last hour explaining to everyone that Santa had been a little tipsy, and they'd be using someone else next year, and yes, it really *was* a disgrace, that sort of thing in front of the children. It seemed to work. No one *really* wanted to believe an ancient version of Santa has just tried to shove a small child into a carnivorous sack in the middle of the Christmas market. The W.I., meanwhile, were handing out the gifts to the children, and DI Adams had heard at least two of them declare that they would like a sword for Christmas so that they could fight

Santa. She wasn't entirely sure who they thought was going to give them a sword, but it seemed to indicate they had their priorities straight.

"I rather think that is it, yes," Beaufort said. "Can't you feel it? The magic's fading."

"What about the faeries?" Miriam asked. "They were most unpleasant!"

"We gave them the old what for," Walter said. "They won't be bothering *you* again."

Gilbert muttered something about thuggish behaviour, and Amelia tweaked his ear.

"Very impressive, that Santa thing," Rose said, tipping her glass of mulled wine to everyone. "Great show, really."

"It wasn't a *show*," Carlotta said. "That little girl almost got eaten!"

"She was *fine*. It'll be character-building."

"Or leave her with a lifetime of expensive therapy bills," Pearl said. "One or the other."

There was a general murmur of agreement at that, and Gert topped up everyone's mulled wine.

"But will everything go back to normal now?" Jasmine asked.

"In this village?" DI Adams asked, and snorted. The ladies all stared at her, and her ears went hot. "I mean, you know …" She took a sip of mulled wine.

"I mean, no more snapping turtles," Jasmine said. "Or aggressive wreaths, or … or swearing lizards in Pearl's chimney."

"Swearing *French* lizards," Pearl said.

"I think most of it will stop," Beaufort said. "It was an overflow of magic, but it's all used up now. You might be stuck with the lizards, though."

"Oh, good," Pearl said.

"But shouldn't there have been drummers?" Miriam asked, and

everyone looked at her. The mulled wine had made her go a little pink. "You know, like in the song. We had geese and milkmaids and pipers and so on. Shouldn't there have been twelve drummers?"

"*Humans,*" Thompson said. "What did I tell you about trying to force patterns on things?"

"I just thought," Miriam said, then gave up. "No. I suppose not."

"Well," Alice said. "I rather think that's enough excitement for one night, even without drummers. Shall we go?"

There was an eruption of movement and chatter in the stall, while the ladies of the Toot Hansell W.I. packed up, offering mince pies to dragons and finishing up the mulled wine and arguing over who got to take the last almond and orange cake home. DI Adams left them to it, going back to the centre of the market. The tree loomed above her, a little singed in places and the baubles replaced somewhat unevenly by the dragons, and the Christmas lights were reflected in the spilled water slicking the cobbles. The stars were high and distant, and somewhere she could hear carol singers, voices rising and falling on the chill air.

She picked up the sack from where she'd left it under the stage. It was a little heavy, but manageable. Dandy whined at her, and looked at the well.

She frowned. "Well, that hardly seems safe. That must be right in the town's water supply."

He huffed, and went to investigate some Christmas pudding he'd missed earlier.

DI Adams shouldered the sack and headed for her car. She'd find somewhere better for it than a town well. That sort of careless behaviour was the exactly the thing that got you ancient, starving Santas.

She whistled for Dandy and he ran after her, dreadlocked hair flying, and Christmas settled over Toot Hansell and the high, distant fells as winter rolled steadily away from the shortest day.

And while the old, wild magic faded, everywhere was magic of a different kind, the magic of carefully chosen but entirely inaccurate (and occasionally inappropriate) gifts, and inexpertly wrapped boxes, and lovingly imperfect meals, and the sweet, shared joys of badly planned days that lit the long, dark nights.

Which is the most beautiful magic of all.

ALMOND, ORANGE & CRANBERRY CAKE

Last year, I discovered a rather lovely orange and cardamom cake that I popped up on the website. It was decorated with a joyful amount of pomegranate seeds, and, since I can never leave a recipe well enough alone, spiked with pomegranate molasses and juice as well. It looked like the perfect celebration cake, and I still adore it.

Only, it's both very sweet and very bitter, due to the two whole oranges you boil to make it. And it takes six eggs, which always seems excessive to me, as I only ever buy six at a time (and they usually last me a good couple of weeks, if not more). And besides, I've already done it. I couldn't do a repeat, even if it was from the blog to the book (the mince pie recipe doesn't count. It's an extra).

So I decided to tweak things.

I wanted this one to be fully gluten-free from the start, so that meant none of the flour from the original recipe, and I wanted to use fewer eggs and fewer oranges (in retrospect, I now see that the breakability of the new cake is down to not having so many eggs to bind it. Which the SO probably would have told me if I'd asked, but never let it be said I've allowed having a chef as a partner get in the way of my cavalier attitude to recipes).

Of course, it still had to taste indulgent and glorious and worthy of dragons, and probably be a bit sticky and messy into the bargain. And freeze well. As you may have gathered by now, I like having a freezer full of baked goods in case of unexpected shortages.

And I feel this ticks all boxes. It's festive, a little softer than the original, and drenched in syrup. It needs no icing, but a little cream would be delightful. Serve it warm and crumbling, or cold and a little tart, with a cuppa on the side.

- 1 large orange
- 75 g / 5 ⅓ Tbsp / 2 ⅔ oz butter, softened
- 200 g / 1 cup soft light brown sugar
- 1 tsp vanilla
- 3 large eggs
- 250 g / 2 ½ cups ground almonds
- 60 g / ½ cup polenta
- ½ tsp salt
- 1 ½ tsp baking powder
- ¼ tsp cardamom (optional)
- ½ tsp grated nutmeg
- 100 g / ¾ cup dried cranberries

For the syrup:

- 60 g / 4 ¾ Tbsp sugar
- 100 mL / just under ½ cup fresh squeezed orange juice
- flaked almonds, lightly toasted, to decorate

Pop the orange in a saucepan with enough water to cover it, and bring it to a low boil. Cook until it's soft. You'll probably need to top up the water, and it'll take about an hour. Allow to cool until you can handle it, then remove the pithy bit around the stem. Blend it in a food processor or blender until reasonably smooth.

Preheat oven to 160°C / 320°F. Butter a springform pan and line the base.

Beat the butter and sugar until it starts to change colour and look a little fluffy. Add the blended orange and beat until well mixed. Add the vanilla, then the eggs one by one, beating just to combine in between each. Add the dry ingredients and beat to just combine, then fold in the cranberries.

Pour into prepared pan and smooth the top gently, then pop in the oven. Bake for about 40 minutes, or until it starts to pull away from the sides.

While it's baking, combine your sugar and juice for the syrup. Keep popping back to stir it now and then, until the sugar is all dissolved.

With the cake out of the oven, leave it in the pan but pop it on a rack on an easy to clean surface or over an oven tray. Stab the top of the cake enthusiastically with a wooden skewer (an excellent way to relieve festive stress), then spoon your syrup generously over the whole thing. Use the lot – it'll pool in places, but absorb eventually. Scatter almonds over the top so they stick to the syrup.

Once cool and set, you can take it out of the tin and get it onto a plate. Be careful – it's heavy and prone to breaking. However, any cracks are easily disguised with cream and a few extra almonds ...

Serves 10.

LATE TO THE PARTY

Miriam's garden was all soft curves and gentle overhangs, the snow of the previous night blurring the sharp edges of leafless trees and empty pots, and giving the familiar shapes of the shrubs mysterious proportions. The brook beyond the garden gate muttered to itself softly, muted by the snowy banks, and the scent of woodsmoke hung sweet and low under the pale afternoon sky.

Mortimer stood on the garden path with the snow melting softly beneath his paws, his closed eyes lifted to the last of the afternoon sun. He was listening, in all the ways creatures listen, with not just his ears but his scales and heart and the pressure of his claws against the frozen ground. But he couldn't hear anything except the brook chuckling as if at a private joke, and somewhere a dog barking. All else was still.

He opened his eyes and sat down, ignoring the chill. His belly was full of Yorkshire puddings and nut roast and lentil roast and mushroom Wellington and gravy, as well as potatoes three ways and cauliflower cheese and stuffing and sprouts and broccoli and …

He burped, and covered his mouth with one paw, looking around guiltily. He thought Miriam might have over-catered slightly. She'd insisted that if DI Collins were coming for Christmas dinner, DI Adams should as well, then promptly panicked about cooking a vegetarian festive meal. Mortimer personally thought she'd done terribly well, although having two roasts *and* a Wellington did seem excessive. And she'd dropped the gravy jug on her foot and broken it when DI Adams knocked on the door, so had ended up serving gravy from an old teapot. Which evidently was not how gravy was meant to be served, but Mortimer failed to see why a teapot was so different to a gravy boat, or why a jug was called a boat in the first place.

A robin hopped across the path, paused to give Mortimer a severe look, then continued on its way. For a moment stillness returned, and Mortimer had time to take a deep, cold breath and think that maybe things would be quieter now. Maybe things could just *stop* for a little, and there could be tea and cake and some work on creating new bauble variations, and nothing else. No investigations. No magical spills. Just a quiet life.

The kitchen door opened behind him, and he turned around to see Beaufort padding out onto the path, his scales steaming as they hit the cold air.

"Hello, lad," the High Lord said, blinking at the marshmallow-y garden. "Everything alright?"

"It seems to be," Mortimer said. "For now, at least."

Beaufort sat down next to him. A lightly singed paper hat was hanging off one of his ears, and he was wearing a tartan scarf that complimented his scales rather nicely. "It's always *for now*, lad. Nothing stays the same forever, whether we consider it to be good or bad. But I didn't mean the village. I meant you."

"Well, no one's been eaten by a tree-dwelling turtle or kidnapped by geese, so that's something."

Beaufort puffed a thoughtful green smoke ring, and it drifted away over the still garden, twisting on itself gently. "That sounds rather worse than what actually happened."

"It's what *could* happen. There's *so much* that could happen – more magic spills, or the Watch coming in, or that journalist writing a big story about us, or … or just *anything*, Beaufort." Mortimer swallowed hard, the afternoon suddenly feeling as if were plunging too quickly into night, the shadows already looming deep and heavy, and his belly far too full.

Beaufort scratched his jaw. "You're quite right, of course. Anything *could* happen. It doesn't mean it will, though. And worrying about it won't change things."

"I can't help it," Mortimer said, and looked at his tail. "We're just sitting around eating *nut roast,* and anything could be coming. I can't stop worrying, and I can't stop *shedding,* and I'm just going to be a nervous, bald dragon *forever.*"

The old dragon was silent, watching the robin as it hopped back across the path, ignoring them. Finally he said, "I imagine someone saying *just stop worrying* is no help whatsoever, then."

Mortimer made a small noise, and poked at a loose scale. It clung on, but only just.

"You could tell me what you're worried about," Beaufort said. "I might not understand, exactly, but I can listen. Might that help?"

Mortimer considered the fact that many of his worries centred around the old dragon's more ambitious ideas, and made another small noise, trying to indicate agreement and disagreement all at once.

"A mince pie, then," Beaufort said. "A mince pie and some tea. You can fix a lot of things with mince pies and tea." He patted Mortimer's shoulder and got up, his paper hat drifting to the ground. "Oh dear." He tried to put it back on, but it slipped over his eyes and fell off again, looking distinctly more singed. "I don't understand the point of these things."

"I'm not sure humans do either," Mortimer said, managing to

hook the hat over a couple of the High Lord's spines. "It's like the sprouts. No one ate them but Gilbert, but apparently they're compulsory."

"Odd sorts, humans," Beaufort said, ambling back to the door. "Lovely, of course, but odd." He looked back at Mortimer. "You don't have to be a Lord, you know."

"I don't?" Mortimer asked, following him.

"Of course not. I think you'd be an excellent Lord, but it's your choice. You do more than enough as it is."

"Oh," Mortimer said, and didn't know what else to say after that.

Beaufort opened the door and heat washed out to greet them. The little, low-beamed kitchen felt even more crowded with the table extended to its full size, still crammed with dishes and jugs and glasses and plates. "The offer stands, of course," the old dragon said, leading the way in. "But I shall find a new Lord in the meantime. We need some younger influence, I think."

"I'll do it," Gilbert said, sitting up from where he was sprawled on the floor, holding his belly. "I'll be a Lord."

"You won't," Amelia said. "You said it was an archaic institution that needs to be abolished."

"I plan to dismantle the system from the inside."

"*Hmm*," Beaufort said. "Maybe when you stop setting birds loose."

"Gilbert! You *said* you wouldn't!" Amelia turned on her brother, and Thompson shot past Mortimer's paws, chasing a bauble. Beaufort had taken it on himself to make his own baubles to give the humans as gifts. They refused to float, and instead just scooted around the floor at unpredictable intervals.

Thompson stopped short and licked a paw, his tail lashing furiously.

"Alright there, Thompson?" Beaufort asked.

"It's these damn *baubles*," the cat said. "They just— *Bollocks!*" He bolted off again as the bauble hurtled past, trailing a thin thread of smoke.

"Cat nature," Miriam said, and put a hand on Mortimer's shoulder. "Would you like a mince pie? I have extra cream."

"Are you alright?" he asked her. "I mean, after everything …?" He couldn't explain it. There was too much to put into words, too many dangers and risks and concerns. But if anyone understood, it would be Miriam.

"Right now? Yes," she said, struggling with the coffee pot. She spilled coffee grounds all over the worktop and threw an alarmed look at DI Adams, then smiled at Mortimer. "I mean, one can't help worrying. But some things help." She nodded at the kitchen.

Mortimer looked around. DI Collins was washing up, his sleeves rolled to the elbows and his face pink, and DI Adams was drying. She looked marginally more comfortable than she had when she had arrived clutching a bottle of wine in one hand and a bag of gifts in the other. A paper hat was perched on top of the tight bundle of her hair, and there was a damp patch on her jumper where she'd spilled gravy, but she snorted when Collins dropped a plate in the sink and set off a sudsy tidal wave. Alice was slicing almond cake at the table into perfect serving sizes, and Dandy was snoring in the best spot in front of the Aga. Thompson was still sprinting after baubles, and Amelia and Gilbert were still arguing, and Beaufort was watching them with amused interest, his paper hat slowly reducing itself to cinders. All was warm, and scented with spice and promise, a bubble of peace as precious as it was fleeting. And something loosened in Mortimer's chest a little, as if he'd had a knot of fire there that just wouldn't go up or come down.

He looked back at Miriam. "Oh," he said. "That's good, then."

"Are *you* alright?" she asked, and he took a moment to think before he answered.

"Yes," he said. "I think I am, actually."

"Good." She offered him a plate. "Mince pie?"

"Please."

It tasted of nutmeg and sugar and something indefinable, and Mortimer took a second one and gave it to Beaufort, who grinned his old, yellow-toothed grin, and said, "Well done, lad."

❄

OUTSIDE, the early night drew in soft and dark, rendering the lights magical where they spilled from windows and wound around trees, and somewhere a very small *boom-boom-boom* started up. It only lasted a moment, then stopped with a soft thud and a squawk. A moment later a tiny figure stood up and shook its fist at the night, then thumped its belly. *Boom-boom-boom.*

Nellie, sitting at the edge of the duckpond, squeezed her snowball and then let it fly. There was another thud, another squawk, and for a moment silence. Then, *boom.*

The sprite hissed softly through her sharp teeth, and said, "You're late."

A defiant *boom-boom-boom* answered her, from more than one tight belly this time.

"No. If there were going to be twelve drummers you should have been here the day before yesterday."

Boom-boom. It sounded slightly put out.

"You missed your chance. Off you go. I've got as many snowballs as I need."

Nothing. No *boom-boom.* Just a rather resentful silence. Then a very small form detached itself from the shadows and marched off across the green, every line of its tiny body radiating fury.

A second form ran after it, waving, and they shouted at each other briefly in very small voices, arms waving in the air. The second one hit its belly – *boom* – and the first pointed at Nellie, made a very rude gesture at the sky, then resumed walking. The second one jumped up and down where it was, gesticulating wildly, and two more ambled out from the undergrowth. They waved as they passed Nellie, and she nodded at them, still working on her snowballs. The second creature tried to stop the others from leaving, hitting its belly a few more times, but they waved him off, and behind them came a crowd of five more creatures, then another three, all waving politely as they went. Nellie nodded again, and watched them grab the protesting creature as it kept trying to hit its belly, and drag it with them.

A moment later the green was empty, nothing but tiny footprints left behind. They could've been made by birds, if one looked at them from the right angle. Nellie looked around for something else to throw snowballs at, then gave up and slid back into the pond.

"That's it, then," she said, to no one in particular, and basked in the glorious, chill silence of the Christmas night, full of quiet lives and warm loves and the promise of longer days to come.

A BEAUFORT SCALES MYSTERY

❄

THANK YOU

Lovely people, thank you so much for joining me in this romp through a distinctly Toot Hansell Christmas. I hope very much that you've enjoyed it, and have already decided which recipes to make for dragons and which are best suited for distracting feathery or scaled intruders (I vote for the sticky buns. They're delicious, but will also keep any intruder very occupied for at least ten minutes).

In between the baking stints, I'd appreciate it hugely if you could take the time to pop a review up on the website of your choice. We need to spread the word about young anti-establishment dragons and the little known other uses of mulled wine, and this seems to be the best way to do it. Plus, reviews are like those sticky buns. Glorious and delightful and vital to the writing process.

And if you'd like to send me a copy of your review, chat about dragons and baked goods, or anything else, drop me a message at kim@kmwatt.com. I'd love to hear from you!

Until next time,

Read on!

SQUABBLING EXES, ECCENTRIC DRAGONS, & OTHER DANGERS

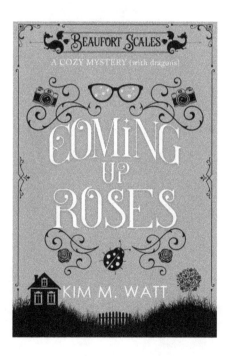

There's a fine line between 'eccentric' and 'a danger to oneself and others'.

And that line may just lie with the body in the freezer.

That's certainly what DI Adams is thinking when said body turns up in Rose's freezer. Of course, the Women's Institute and the dragons have other ideas ...

Grab *Coming Up Roses* today to discover just how far the dragons and the W.I. will go to protect one of their own - and just what Lord Walter is really up to ...

Scan above or head to books2read.com/ComingUpRoses to continue the adventure!

GET THE RECIPES HERE!

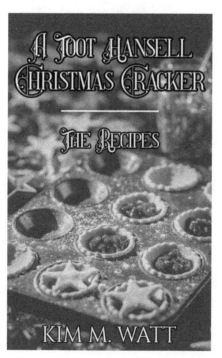

In case you'd like to keep your book clean ...

Should you wish to avoid being distracted by rampaging water fowl and furious faeries (remember to say it with an 'ae') while cooking, and to avoid the rick of a pudding/book disaster, you can grab your recipes as a separate volume right here.

Plus, if this is your first visit to Toot Hansell and/or my newsletter, I'm also going to send you some story collections - including one about how that whole barbecue thing started ...

Your free recipe collection is waiting - grab it now!

Happy baking!

Scan above to grab your recipes in ebook, or head to https:// readerlinks.com/l/2369428/xcpb and download them now!

ABOUT THE AUTHOR

Hello lovely person. I'm Kim, and in addition to the Beaufort Scales stories I write other funny, magical books that offer a little escape from the serious stuff in the world and hopefully leave you a wee bit happier than you were when you started. Because happiness, like friendship, matters.

I write about baking-obsessed reapers setting up baby ghoul petting cafes, and ladies of a certain age joining the Apocalypse on their Vespas. I write about friendship, and loyalty, and lifting each other up, and the importance of tea and cake.

But mostly I write about how wonderful people (of all species) can really be.

If you'd like to find out the latest on new books in *The Beaufort Scales* series, as well as discover other books and series, giveaways, extra reading, and more, jump on over to www.kmwatt.com and check everything out there.

Read on!

amazon.com/Kim-M-Watt/e/B07JMHRBMC
bookbub.com/authors/kim-m-watt
facebook.com/KimMWatt
instagram.com/kimmwatt
twitter.com/kimmwatt

ACKNOWLEDGMENTS

To you, lovely reader. Because there would be no dragons without you. You are all entirely wonderful, and your messages, social media chats, and just general delightful reader-ish-ness make this all worthwhile. Thank you.

To Lynda Dietz at Easy Reader Editing, without whom I would have have committed far more cardinal grammar sins than I do already. All mistakes are mine. All credit for not using "festive" in every second sentence goes to her.

And, always, to the SO, who suffers me ruining his recipes on a regular basis and yet still offers ideas and advice for Yorkshire-specific baked goods. I will learn to follow a recipe one day. Maybe.

ALSO BY KIM M. WATT

The Beaufort Scales Series (cozy mysteries with dragons)

"The addition of covert dragons to a cozy mystery is perfect...and the dragons are as quirky and entertaining as the rest of the slightly eccentric residents of Toot Hansell."

– Goodreads reviewer

The Gobbelino London, PI series

"This series is a wonderful combination of humor and suspense that won't let you stop until you've finished the book. Fair warning, don't plan on doing anything else until you're done ..."

- Goodreads reviewer

Short Story Collections

Oddly Enough: Tales of the Unordinary, Volume One

"The stories are quirky, charming, hilarious, and some are all of the above without a dud amongst the bunch ..."

- Goodreads reviewer

The Tales of Beaufort Scales

A collection of dragonish tales from the world of Toot Hansell, as a welcome gift for joining the newsletter! Just mind the abominable snow porcupine … (you can head to www.kmwatt.com to find a link to join)

The Cat Did It

Of course the cat did it. Sneaky, snarky, and up to no good - that's the cats in this feline collection which you can grab free via the newsletter (it'll automatically arrive on soft little cat feet in your inbox not long after the *Tales* do). Just remember - if the cat winks, always wink back …

www.ingramcontent.com/pod-product-compliance
Lightning Source LLC
LaVergne TN
LVHW050741020225
802648LV00011B/187